THE
ISLAND

Also by
Will Overby

The Killing Vision

The Human Condition:
Short Fiction and Poetry

Drum

August

THE

ISLAND

A NOVEL OF TERROR

WILL OVERBY

DAWSON SPRINGS, KENTUCKY
2013

ISBN-13: 978-0615894744
ISBN-10: 0615894747

I

TEA AND SYMPATHY

T he first time Robert appeared was six months after the accident that killed him.

It was Sarah's Tuesday afternoon Intro to Anthropology class. The early spring sun streamed through the windows of her classroom, the afternoon air was alive with the hum of insects and birds, and she had just launched into a dissertation on race and biological differences to a group of bored freshmen. She took a breath to start a sentence and there he was.

He stood in the back corner of the room, leaning against the wall with his thumbs tucked into his pockets and smiling at her with that crooked grin that melted her heart the first time she'd gone out with him. She stared dumbly back at him, her mouth open and slack. Robert was wearing a brown tweed sports jacket, and she remembered it was the one he'd been buried in. She studied the curve of his jaw, his soft brown hair. She could even see the steel blue of his eyes. The vision suddenly blurred and she realized her eyes were starting to water.

"Miss Dunham?"

Sarah looked toward the voice. Kelsie Thompson, one of the brighter girls in the class. Kelsie was watching her closely. In fact, all of them were staring at her. The room had gone deadly silent.

Kelsie cleared her throat. "Miss Dunham, are you okay?"

Sarah glanced back at the corner. Robert was gone.

She smiled at Kelsie. "I'm fine," she said. She rubbed her temples. "I'm all right." She realized the students were still watching her. Their faces swam before her, and she leaned back against the desk. "Let's go ahead and break for today," she said, closing her eyes. "I'm not feeling very well."

Everyone began shuffling their books and papers and filing out the classroom door. Kelsie stopped and placed a hand on Sarah's arm.

Sarah gave her a tight smile. "I'll be okay. Thank you."

She stood motionless until Kelsie was gone and the room was blessedly quiet. She stared at the corner where Robert had been. Had she really seen him?

She gathered her books and papers, took one last glance at the corner, and turned out the lights on her way through the door. The hallway was empty as other classes droned on behind closed doors. Her footsteps echoed on the tile as she made her way to her office, grateful for the lack of students. She really didn't think she could face anyone right now.

She slipped through the Anthropology/Sociology Department door, trying to make as little noise as possible. Amy Vandiver, the associate professor in the office next door, would want to yap. Sarah flipped on the lights in her office and promptly hung the toe of her shoe on the leg of a chair, knocking it against the wall.

"Sarah?"

"It's me."

"Your class over already?"

Sarah placed her material on her desk and rounded the corner between the two offices, plastering what she hoped was a pleasant expression on her face. "I let out a little early today. Wasn't feeling well."

Amy pulled a strand of curly auburn hair behind her ear. "You don't *look* well."

Sarah thought of Robert standing in the corner of the classroom, of how clearly she could see his eyes. "I'm okay."

Amy set her pen down and leaned back in her chair. "So what's up? You want some tea?" Amy kept an electric kettle in her office. It was always full.

Sarah didn't really want anything, but she found herself nodding as she sank into the chair opposite Amy.

Amy pulled a cup from the shelf and filled it with steaming water, then slid it across the desk with a teabag. "Sugar?"

"Sure."

Amy pulled a white packet out of a drawer. "You sure you're okay?"

Sarah dunked the teabag into her cup. "I just saw Robert."

Amy froze. "You what?"

Sarah kept her eyes on the teabag as it went up and down. "I saw Robert."

"Sarah. . ."

She felt the tears spilling down her face before she realized she was crying. "He was there. In the classroom. Just standing there."

Amy's hand covered hers. It was warm and dry. Her brown eyes were round with concern. "You know that's not possible."

Sarah grabbed a tissue from the box on Amy's desk and dabbed at her eyes. "I know. Believe me, I know." She felt stupid now that she was away from the classroom, now that she was sitting here in Amy's cozy office with a warm cup of tea and looking at her friend across the desk. "I'm sorry," she said. "I didn't mean to lose it." She felt like an idiot, telling Amy she had seen her dead fiancé in her classroom. What would Amy think of her?

Amy squeezed Sarah's hand. "It's okay, Sarah," she said. "I know it's been a rough few months."

Sarah felt a spark of anger at Amy's words. Amy had no idea how rough it had been – the accident, losing Robert, the weeks of physical therapy. The sudden sense of isolation and loneliness. The stares and whispers of students and colleagues that followed her as she made her way across campus. Part of her wanted to spill all this out to Amy, to punish her for her pity. Instead she simply nodded.

Amy gave her a soft smile. "You ever think maybe you came back too soon?"

"Maybe." In truth, Sarah wondered this daily. The beginning of the spring semester – which now seemed a lifetime ago – overwhelmed her at first, and she struggled to keep up with all her classes. Grading assignments and tests took twice as long as it had before the accident and she became short-tempered with some of the students, especially the freshmen and others in the Intro class who were only there for the general education credit. That wasn't like her at all.

She'd always prided herself on her compassion and patience, but now during some of her exchanges with students she felt as if she were watching herself from outside, a stranger watching a movie.

Dr. Flores told her this was normal, that she would go through these feelings as part of the grieving process, explained how the brain worked through these emotions even as he prescribed pills to dull them. She wondered if taking the pills was a mistake, if maybe she should just let her brain do its job, if using the medication only prolonged the healing process. But then he was the doctor, and she supposed she needed to do as he instructed.

Amy leaned back in her chair. "Maybe you should go on home. Get some rest."

Sarah nodded and dabbed eyes again. She had a stack of essays to grade, but that could be done at home. She took a sip of her tea. It was hot and bitter, and she realized she hadn't used the sugar packet Amy had given her. "I think I might just do that." She was suddenly very tired and a dull ache throbbed in her temples. She looked down at her full cup. "I'm afraid I didn't drink much of my tea."

"Don't worry about it," Amy said. She gave a small smile.

Sarah gritted her teeth and pulled herself out of the chair. "Thanks for listening."

"Hey," Amy said, "tea and sympathy is what we're all about here at Cedar Hill State College."

Sarah couldn't help but laugh. "We should put that on a t-shirt."

2

Amy watched Sarah slink out of the doorway, and then in a couple of minutes, heard her lock up her office and leave. She let out a long breath and leaned back in her chair, watching the steam rise from Sarah's cup of tea. Sarah exuded sadness like an odor, and Amy was always drained after their conversations.

Not that she wasn't sympathetic. She could only imagine what it was like to lose your fiancé, your *soul mate*, just before your wedding. She recalled Sarah in the months and weeks prior to the accident, how energetic and full of life she was. How happy and excited. It was like remembering a different person. At the time Amy would listen to Sarah's bouncing descriptions of dresses and invitations and flowers like the dutiful coworker she was, interjecting her comments in all the appropriate places, but secretly wishing Sarah would just shut the fuck up. There was nothing as tiring as hearing about someone else's wedding. Unless it was hearing about their kids.

Amy grabbed Sarah's cup and carried it down the hall to the ladies' room, poured the tea into the sink and rinsed it out.

She knew her feelings about Sarah's wedding were just misplaced jealousy. She was honest enough with herself to admit that. It was hard as hell watching your friend plan her dream wedding when your own was several years behind you and stained by a bitter divorce.

She ripped a couple of paper towels from the holder and wiped out the cup. Just the thought of Tim was enough to send her into a murderous rage. But she wouldn't think about that today. She wouldn't give him the satisfaction of ruining her evening.

She peeked through the window into Sarah's office on the way back to her own. In the darkness she could barely make out the knickknacks on the shelves – souvenirs and keepsakes from Sarah's numerous trips abroad. A carved African mask loomed in the shadows, its black eyes sending a shiver up Amy's spine. Below that was a brightly painted boomerang from Australia dotted with aboriginal depictions of birds and kangaroos. Sarah was well-traveled, which helped fuel her passion for anthropology. Amy had only been out of the country once, on her honeymoon with Tim to St. Martin, and she couldn't help but smile at the memory of the two of them cavorting on the secluded clothing-optional beach near their bungalow.

She smacked her palm against the doorframe. Dammit, why did Tim have to fuck up everything? She hadn't seen or spoken to him in three years, since she began her assistant professorship here at Cedar Hill, but he always lurked in the back of her mind, ready to make an appearance at the most inopportune time.

Back at her desk she stacked up the term papers she had been grading and banded them together. There were still at least ten more to go through. She sighed and picked up the next one. "Gender Inequality in the Modern United States." She didn't know if she could take one more feminist manifesto written by a student just discovering herself.

Even as she read, her mind kept wandering back to Sarah. And Sarah's vision of Robert. That was troubling. She knew Sarah was seeing a psychiatrist and taking prescription meds. Could any of the drugs cause hallucinations? Sarah seemed so fragile since she had come back. It might not take much to send her reeling over the edge. Amy would have to keep a closer eye on her.

She blew out a breath and turned back to the paper in front of her. She wanted to finish these before her evening class at six. It was looking like a long evening.

3

Sarah slowed the Honda as she approached home – the Victorian at 1450 Cantrell Lane. She never failed to be awed by the sight of the house as it rose up from behind the trees lining the street. From the wide front porch with its gingerbread trim to the tiny eye-like windows of the third floor attic, the place exuded charm and dignity. The shrubs out front were full and green, and in the side yard the azaleas were dripping with lush, pink blossoms. If only Robert were still here to take pride in his and Sarah's hard work at restoring the house.

She pulled into the drive – if it could be called a drive. It was really two concrete runners that went from the street back to the tiny detached garage. No doubt the drive and garage were additions in the mid-1920s, built for Model Ts and petite roadsters. She and Robert had often joked about the driveway and how it was such a mismatch for his Explorer. But she wouldn't think about the Explorer now, because every time she did it was accompanied by the sound of screeching tires and shattering glass.

She stopped by the back door and climbed out, grabbing her tote bag and her empty Starbucks cup from the morning. The sun was warm and comforting on her face and shoulders, and she stood for a moment with her eyes closed, breathing in the fresh spring air and listening to the chatter of birds all around her. Somewhere along the next street children squealed with laughter, and she felt a pang of hurt in her chest. But it was nice out. Maybe after dinner she would bring out a glass of wine and grade her essays on the patio.

Inside the back door, she dropped her tote on the kitchen table and threaded her way through the house to the double front doors to check the mail. The only thing in the box was an electronics catalog addressed to Robert, which she dropped in the trash when she returned to the kitchen. She pulled a pizza from the freezer and turned on the oven to preheat while she changed clothes. She really ought to walk on the treadmill, but she didn't think she could do it today. She was exhausted, both physically and emotionally. In the living room, she turned on the TV and set it to the big band music channel, and soon Glenn Miller echoed through the dark halls of the house.

Upstairs she slipped out of her work clothes and pulled on a pair of sweats and an old t-shirt. She started toward the bathroom with her dirty clothes when her gaze lit on the portrait of Robert and her on the dresser. Their engagement portrait. Robert handsome in his gray suit and smiling that grin of his into the camera, Sarah with her head resting against his chest, her blonde hair perfectly curled and coiffed. They looked so happy, so innocent. Tears brimmed in her eyes as she thought how six weeks after the picture was taken, Robert was gone. She sank down onto the edge of the bed, still staring at the photograph through bleary eyes until she heard the oven beep downstairs.

Benny Goodman was playing up a storm over the TV as she descended the stairs, and she thought of the times she and Robert had danced in the living room. She could still see him sliding over the wood floors in his sock feet, his hair flying about on his head, a silly grin plastered on his face.

She could not stop thinking about the vision she'd had in the classroom. Robert standing there in the corner. Looking as solid as any real human being. Looking at her with those intense blue eyes.

Wearing his funeral clothes.

She shuddered and unwrapped the pizza. She knew it had just been an illusion, probably some hallucination brought on by exhaustion and medication. She'd been going full throttle all semester. Throwing herself into work seemed a logical way to work out her grief – even Dr. Flores had said so. But she wondered, as Amy had, whether she had gone back too soon. There were moments, standing before her classes or talking with colleagues, when she would just blank out in mid-sentence. The doctors warned her this might happen, a result of her minor head injury, but it always embarrassed her, and she felt like a bumbling fool. She wondered if the frustration she felt at such times was similar to what older people felt in the beginning stages of dementia. But she had never hallucinated before. Had never had a vision so clear and convincing as what she had seen today. She had seen the individual threads in Robert's tweed jacket.

His funeral jacket.

She pulled a bottle of Woodbridge white zinfandel from the refrigerator and opened it with a satisfying *pluck*, then poured herself a full glass. Robert's favorite wine. He'd wanted a special wine cooler for the kitchen when they remodeled it, but she told him it was a silly luxury. They were already over budget from the plumbing problems in the upstairs bathroom and they had a wedding to pay for. Not to mention their hoped-for honeymoon in Cozumel. Now she felt guilty for denying him his one request in the whole renovation. A freaking wine cooler. How much would it have been, three hundred dollars? Four hundred? A small price to pay to have seen the smile on his face one more time.

As the pizza baked, she carried her wine out the back door and down onto the patio and melted into one of the chairs around the firepit table. She turned her face toward the setting sun and took a sip of wine, letting the coolness trickle down her throat. She loved it here, this neighborhood, one of the older established areas of Cedar Hill. So quiet and peaceful. She and Robert had driven through here often on Sunday afternoons, looking at the houses and daydreaming, never imagining any of these homes would be within their reach. So when the house came on the market she half-heartedly called the realtor to inquire the asking price, more to satisfy her curiosity than anything else. And when she realized they could afford it, she was over the moon. She dragged a reluctant Robert to a showing, and although the interior was dark and dusty and the siding needed a new coat of paint, she could tell Robert was as in love with the place as she was. They both lay awake all night talking about it, and the next morning they called with an offer. That evening when the realtor showed up at their doorstep to tell them the offer had been accepted, Sarah and Robert kissed each other and jumped up and down like silly school kids.

They spent the night here the day they signed the papers, making love and sleeping in a tangle of sheets thrown over the hardwood floor. Those first few weeks were a blur of stripping old wallpaper and painting, of cleaning lacquered wood molding and scrubbing ancient bath fixtures. And making love. Always making love. Though they had been living together in an apartment for two years, it was as if the house awakened something within them, something that pushed their libidos into overdrive. They could not get enough of each other. Even during her long days at the college, she found herself wanting him, eager for the late afternoon when she could make the drive across town and offer herself to him. And Robert, man that he was, never refused. She had to smile when she thought of all the nights they skipped dinner and spent the evening in bed. How she would cling to him, how he would moan as he slipped over the edge. . .

He was wearing his funeral clothes.

A breeze wound across the patio, sharp and cold. She shivered. The wine glass was like ice in her hand.

By the time she reached her apartment, Amy was hungry enough to gnaw the countertop in the kitchen. She had finished up grading the term papers at 5:30, and grabbed a candy bar from the vending machine down the hall on her way to class. The class, Sociology and American Religion, nearly degenerated into chaos as a discussion on political views and religious tolerance quickly became an argument between two young men – one a Christian and the other an outspoken Wiccan. Amy was accustomed to such events in this class. Religion was such a personal subject that students often felt offended during the discussions of various beliefs. Some people became outraged, as if the consideration of other religions was an affront to their own faiths. For herself, a lapsed Baptist and a sociologist, the arguments both fascinated and amused her. She had learned over the past few semesters how to even out tempers and reduce these kinds of flare-ups, but this class seemed to fan the flames of intolerance like no other she taught.

She pulled a carton of leftovers from the refrigerator, the remains of Chinese takeout, and popped it into the microwave. She had never been one for cooking, and the evenings she had night classes she barely even felt like nuking anything. Last Wednesday night she had come home and devoured half a can of cocktail peanuts and a beer.

The episode with Sarah still concerned her. Amy thought about her rattling around that old house of hers like a ghost and wondered if she should give her a call, just to check on her. But Sarah had made it clear when she came back to work that she didn't need anyone hovering over her; in fact, she sent her own mother packing back to Springfield a week after Robert's funeral. Sarah was an odd bird. She wanted so fiercely to be independent, but Amy could see her resolve slowly ebbing away, as if Robert's death was leeching the life out of her.

She remembered the feeling of being utterly and hopelessly in love with someone – with Tim – as if life itself depended on eating, sleeping and breathing him. And she supposed if Tim had been ripped from her in those early days that she would have known the pain and loss as deeply as Sarah did.

But for his part, Tim turned out to be an asshole. The petty arguments had been easily forgotten at first, back when they were in the throes of honeymoon lust. But as time went on, Tim's criticisms of her housekeeping and cooking, his little barbs directed at her driving habits, and even his half-serious comments about her religious studies began to drive her insane. They both knew it was over long before they parted and she left

Houston for the little private college in Cedar Hill, a thousand miles away. The last she had heard of him, his management consulting business had really taken off and he was hiring five extra people to balance the workload. That was three years ago. She really didn't have any ill will toward him; in fact, she hoped his business would continue to be successful. But she had no desire to ever see him again.

At least that's what she told herself. And then she would find herself thinking of him again and she would be filled with anger and revulsion.

There was no doubt her split from Tim had been good for her, although in those early weeks right after the divorce she found herself in the midst of behavior she never would have engaged in before her marriage. For one thing, there had been men. Several men. It was as though she couldn't be sated. She craved sex like a drug, and when the longing hit her she couldn't stop until she'd had her fix. Sometimes she felt like a test subject in her own sociological experiment, and she would watch herself dispassionately move from one relationship to another, sickeningly fascinated with herself.

And with the sex came the booze. Not that she had a problem with alcohol, but during that time she was overindulging in everything and she wasn't about to turn down drinks. Especially when they were being provided by hunky guys she couldn't wait to get in bed with. One night during a bout of heavy drinking she wound up in a tattoo parlor with a Celtic triskele symbol on the back of her neck just below her hairline. That was when she made a conscious decision to slow down.

Coming to Cedar Hill seemed the perfect opportuni-

ty to turn her life around. It was a small college town
on the northern fringes of the Bible Belt; close enough
to have a backbone of conservatism, but far enough
away that you could still grab a beer on Sunday afternoon if you needed one. The college itself was tiny –
five main buildings and a single co-ed dormitory
around a sprawling quad. It was a private liberal arts
college, expensive and exclusive with only fifteen hundred students – only a third of that number during the
summer sessions. It was the perfect place to get away
from her past and reinvent herself.

Which was why meeting and working with Sarah
had been so liberating. Sarah had never slept around or
drifted through innumerable drunken stupors or woken
up on the couches of strangers with no recollection of
how she'd gotten there. Sarah still went to mass every
Sunday. Sarah was a good girl, someone Amy felt she
could emulate. She was happy. And she had guided
Amy through the ins and outs of the college hierarchy,
helped her set up her schedule, and even tried to set her
up on a few dates. Sarah and Robert had both been
good friends to her, although sometimes Amy felt like a
fifth wheel when she was with them. It was easy to see
they were deeply in love, which made the failure of
Amy's marriage that much more painful. Which made
Sarah's excitement over her upcoming wedding hard to
take.

Amy felt an overpowering guilt at how she had
treated Sarah just before the accident, when she felt that
if she had to hear one more word about that fucking
dress she was going to snap. She distanced herself
from Sarah, even as Sarah asked her to be the maid of
honor, even as Sarah confided to Amy her hopes and
fears about marriage and begged Amy to relay the story

of her divorce. But Amy knew once Sarah was married their friendship would turn a corner. Because with marriage came family and kids and soccer practice and all the things Amy had no desire for or interest in. The old Sarah would be gone forever.

Except that never happened. Instead, *Robert* was gone forever, and the old Sarah, the one Amy had grown to love, turned into an empty shell.

She really should do something with Sarah. Something fun. Something that would get her mind off Robert. Maybe the two of them could go somewhere together. The end of the semester was quickly approaching, and they would have a couple of weeks off before the summer sessions started.

The microwave beeped and Amy pulled out her steaming plate, carried it over to the dining table and fired up her laptop. She had an idea, but she needed to do some research first. If it panned out, it would be the trip of a lifetime.

5

She was asleep.

She knew she was asleep because she was floating. It was night, and she was floating through a garden. Trellises heavy with roses of all colors lined the path in the bright moonlight. They were old fashioned tea roses, the ones with the tiny petals, like her grandmother used to have at her house in Memphis. The scent was overwhelming – sweet and heady and suffocating. Farther along where the path intersected three others was a large fountain illuminated by blue spotlights. A stream of water shot from the stone mouth of an angel at the top. She could hear the water trickling from the top basin into the larger one beneath it. The angel's eyes were white and blank.

"Sarah."

She recognized Robert's voice before she turned and saw him. He was standing in the shadows, just out of the reach of the moonlight. "Robert?"

"Sarah."

She moved toward him. "I saw you today," she said. "You came back to me. You came back to see me."

He held his hand out into the pale light. "I love you, Sarah."

She drew closer, close enough to brush his fingertips with her own, then close enough to grab his hand. It was cold and waxy. She could see the cuff of the tweed jacket.

His funeral clothes.

She pulled him closer to the edge of the light, his face still hidden in the darkness. His hands. His hands were covered in dirt. As if...

As if he had clawed his way out of the grave.

Suddenly she didn't want to see his face. She didn't want to see what he had become. She didn't want to see the dead, pale thing that was inching its way out of the darkness into the patch of moonlight. If only she could wake up! If only she could get out of the dream. She opened her mouth to scream, hoping the sound would jar her out of her sleep. But nothing would come out. And Robert was coming closer. Closer. . .

She opened her eyes and found herself staring at the ceiling of the bedroom. The fan blades whirred softly and the air was cold on her clammy skin. Her gown was soaked through with sweat. She sat up, her heart hammering in her chest. The clock said 2:17. She could still smell roses.

A dream. Thank God, it was just a dream. But she couldn't stop thinking about Robert's fingers, the dirt on his hands. The cold, lifeless feel of his skin.

In the darkness, she slipped out of the bed and fumbled her way to the dresser and pulled out a clean gown, then wriggled out of the soiled one, shivering in the chill from the fan. She had just poked her head through the gown when she heard a slight thump above her head in the attic. It was so quiet that she wasn't sure if she had actually heard it or only imagined it in the last vestiges of her disturbing dream. But then she heard a creak, very low, as if someone had taken a step and was trying hard to be quiet about it.

She stood frozen, halfway in her gown, and her heart began pound again. Was someone up there? Should she call the police? With that thought she pushed on into her gown, then wrapped her robe about her. She stood like a stone, her ears straining for the slightest sound. There was nothing.

She had just started to take off her robe and climb back in bed when she heard the creak again. Louder this time. This time she knew it was real.

She thought of Robert's voice, soothing her right after they had moved in, when odd noises would wake her sometimes at night. *It's an old house, Sarah. It's going to make weird sounds. Old pipes, settling floorboards. Maybe a mouse or two. It's just part of the package.* Then he would pull her close and she would settle into the crook of his arm and drift back to sleep. Safe and assured that all was well.

But now Robert wasn't here. And that noise in the attic grated right into her marrow. And the thought of Robert's dirt-stained fingers was fresh in her mind.

She reached out her shaking hand and turned on the bedside lamp. It seemed painfully dim in the darkness of the bedroom. In the drawer of the table was a small flashlight. She grabbed it. Mercifully, the batteries were good and the beam came on strong and bright.

In the hallway she switched on the ceiling light, and she squinted in the sudden brightness. The access ladder to the attic was at the end of the hallway in the ceiling. She headed for it. By now her heart was pounding so hard she was seeing flashing lights with every beat.

I shouldn't be doing this. I should just go call the cops.

And tell them what? That something –

her dead fiancé

– was creeping around in her attic? And then let them come all the way out here and search the house from top to bottom and not find so much as a rat turd? That would be just the thing to cement her reputation as the pitiful thing who lost her future husband and her mind in the same year.

With a sudden burst of courage she walked purposefully to the end of the hall and reached up to the access door, then pulled it open. The ancient ladder slid down and hit the hardwood floor with a solid clunk. This was it. She was going in. She would prove to herself there was nothing to be afraid of. That she was a strong, independent woman.

The steps gave a dry squeak as she climbed up, and the flashlight beam disappeared into the expansive void of the attic overhead. She reached the top and stuck her head through the opening. Except for the two tiny windows on the very back wall the space was pitch black. She aimed the flashlight in front of her.

Robert sat in an old rocking chair facing her. His cold blue eyes were like ice as they stared at her. His skin was sallow and pale.

She screamed and clenched her eyes shut as she fell backwards down the ladder. She hit the floor with a bone-jarring thud. She could only lie there, gasping for breath and writhing in pain. Had she really seen him? Was he really there? She was terrified to open her eyes, imagining that cold dead face peering down at her from the attic opening.

After a moment, she forced her eyes open. She was lying on the floor. The back of her head ached where it had bounced off the hardwood.

In a panic, she grabbed for the flashlight and shone it up at the ceiling. The attic opening was dark and empty.

Was he still up there?

He was wearing his funeral clothes.

She sat up and her head swam. She steadied herself against the wall and slowly climbed to her feet. She had to go back up. She had to see.

Her heart hammered in her chest, and she could hear the blood pulsing in her ears.

She placed one hand on the ladder and started up. Her legs were rubbery and her bowels felt thick and hot. She didn't want to do this, she did not.

You have to.

She climbed higher, aiming the flashlight ahead of her like a sword. The beam was playing over the rafters now. She could see cobwebs dancing from them.

With one last burst of strength, she plunged upward into the open space and shined the light ahead of her.

The rocking chair was empty. The wooden headrest was carved into a sunburst pattern, and she realized she must have been so upset by her dream that she had projected Robert's face onto it. She shined the light all around the attic. Just some dusty boxes. Nothing more.

She was suddenly very weak and nauseated. She managed to descend the ladder safely and make it to the bathroom before the vomit spewed forth. When she was done she sank onto the floor and leaned back against the clawfoot tub. The porcelain was cold and soothing against her shoulders.

Before she could stop them, hot tears coursed down her face. Her gut clenched in dread. She was cracking up. She was seeing things. Hearing things.

You saw him, Sarah.

No! She was still dreaming. Awake and dreaming.

He was real.

She pressed her fists against her face. He *was not* real. She had to convince herself of that. No matter how she felt, how clearly she had seen him, he wasn't there. Robert was dead and in the ground at Our Lady of Peace Gardens. And the dead didn't come back to life. Everyone knew that.

Using the side of the tub, she pulled herself to her feet and flipped on the bathroom light. She squinted in the blinding brilliance, and as her eyes adjusted she saw her hollow-eyed reflection gazing back at her. God, she looked horrible.

She found the pills Dr. Flores had given her for moments such as this. She hadn't had to take them often, and the bottle was still mostly full. She swallowed one down and chased it with a gulp of cold water, then rinsed her face and patted it dry with a towel.

Back in the hallway she slid the ladder back up and let the attic door swing closed. She retrieved the flashlight from a corner of the hallway and switched it off, then turned out the rest of the lights and made her way back to the bedroom. The bedside lamp still burned. She flipped it off and crawled back into the bed.

Again she stared into the darkness, at the fan blades spinning above her head, willing the pill to kick in and bring her blessed oblivion. But each time sleep started to overtake her, Robert's face swam before her, and she jolted awake. Finally, at four o'clock she dragged herself out of bed and downstairs to make coffee and await the gray light of early dawn. There would be no more sleep tonight.

6

Amy had spent the whole evening on the internet and the majority of the morning on the phone with the travel agent. It had been a tough sell with the agent, holding reservations without a deposit until Amy had a chance to confirm everything with Sarah, but he finally agreed to it. Amy was a woman after all, even if she was trying harder to be good, and she still had the old feminine charm to pull out when the situation required it.

A few months before she and Tim split, they had begun planning a trip to the Bahamas. It was a last-ditch effort to salvage their relationship. Amy had researched all the options, including pricing luxury accommodations at the Atlantis Resort in Nassau. Everything she looked at was either ridiculously overpriced or riddled with horrible ratings on the travel websites. But they all had one thing in common: they were crowded. And while saving her marriage was at the top of her list of priorities, surrounding themselves with a sea of humanity while they were in crisis mode didn't appeal to either one of them.

So in desperation she called the travel agency, and the cheerful girl on the other end of the line told her about Ben Harbour on St. Celine, a tiny remote island only accessible by boat from Nassau. "No one really knows about it," the agent said. "It's one of the best kept secrets of the Bahamas. The pictures I've seen are beautiful, and our clients who have stayed there just rave about it."

"We're wanting some alone time," Amy said.

"You'll get it," the agent told her, and something in her voice said she knew exactly what Amy meant. "Most of the inns and hotels in Ben Harbour have their own private beaches. Very quiet."

She and Tim split up before the trip rolled around, but Amy never forgot the agent's description of the island. She had held onto all the travel brochures and literature with the promise that one day she would go there, a tropical paradise with nothing to do all day but lie on the beach.

And it looked like the time was now. Sarah would love it there, too. And it was just what she needed to get her mind off Robert and all she had been through the past few months.

Amy had just hung up the phone with the travel agent when she heard Sarah unlocking her office next door. She gathered her notes and the brochures and swung around the corner just as Sarah flipped on the lights. "Hey."

7

Sarah sat on the patio staring into the deepening twilight. Her wine glass was empty and the breeze that caressed her face was warm and soothing. From the open kitchen window floated the music from the big band channel – Benny Goodman's "Goody-Goody." She didn't understand why she tortured herself with this music. Listening to it always brought back memories of Robert, always ended up making her sad and depressed, no matter how upbeat and bouncy the songs were.

She knew she was sitting out here because she was afraid to go into the house. Robert's face – the one she thought she had seen in the attic, all yellow and dead – floated before her and she shivered in spite of the velvet breeze. She was cracking up. She had to be. No matter the therapy sessions with Dr. Flores. No matter the medication. Ghosts did not exist, and if she was seeing one then something was wrong with her.

Which was why she was considering Amy's invitation.

This morning Amy had appeared in her office doorway, flushed and expectant, just as Sarah arrived for the day. There was a flash of concern in Amy's eyes when their gazes locked, but it vanished in an instant. Sarah knew how awful she appeared; there were dark circles beneath her eyes and she looked – felt – as though she hadn't slept in days. The horrors of last night hadn't helped. She managed a weak smile. "Good morning." She plopped her purse and totebag down on the desk. "You look especially perky today."

"I've got a surprise for you," Amy said. "Just hear me out before you say no."

Sarah looked at her. "What have you been up to?"

Amy fell back into the chair opposite Sarah's desk. "Look, I know this semester's been really rough on you. I know you've had a hard time the past few months. And I know it's probably been lonely over there in that big old house all by yourself."

Sarah wanted to laugh. Amy had no idea. "You're not going to try to fix me up with someone are you?" She knew this was bound to happen sooner or later. Friends and family had good intentions, and she couldn't fault them for that, but a relationship was the last thing she needed right now.

"No!" Amy cried. She held up her hands. "It's nothing like that. I just want to do something fun with you." She shifted on the chair and Sarah knew how uncomfortable she must be; her students hated that seat and usually squirmed the whole time they were in her office. "Did I ever tell you about the trip Tim and I were planning just before we split up?"

Sarah shook her head. "No."

"There's a little island in the Bahamas, St. Celine. Ever heard of it?"

"I don't believe so."

"Hardly anyone has. It's really remote." Amy spread a brochure out on the desk and they studied the bright photos of immaculate pink sand beaches, towering waterfalls and colorful buildings. "The only access is by boat from Nassau. It's very small and very private. It looks beautiful."

Sarah sank into her chair. "So. . . why are you telling me about this?"

"How would you like to go there? With me?"

Sarah gaped at her. "To St. Celine?"

"Yes!"

A million things flashed through her mind. She had to admit, excitement rippled through her at the thought of a few days in a tropical paradise. But she couldn't just take off on a vacation. She had too much to do, too much still to catch up on.

Like what?

It wasn't as if she had kids to care for. Or pets. And summer sessions wouldn't start until June fifteenth; there would be over a month between terms.

Amy was staring at her expectantly. "Come on, Sarah, what do you say? Just us girls. It'll be a blast."

Sarah rubbed her temples. If only she could think straight. If only she wasn't so tired. "I'll have to think about it," she said.

"Of course," Amy said.

And now Sarah sat in the gathering gloom and wondered again about leaving. Maybe it was exactly what she needed. Maybe she had stayed cooped up in this house and cloistered at the college for much too long. It was no wonder she was seeing things. She needed this trip. She needed it to get back her sanity.

She left the patio and stepped into the golden warmth of the house. Benny Goodman had given way to Frank Sinatra, and she giggled as she thought of that old Warner Brothers cartoon where Frank was depicted as a crooning rooster and all the hens in the barnyard were swooning and crying, "Frankie!"

She poured herself another glass of wine and sat down at the bar between the kitchen and dining room. Her laptop still hummed where she had left it after checking her email just before dinner. There was a new message from Amy:

> Hey Girl,
>
> No rush, but I forgot to tell you that I will need to know something in a couple of days. The travel agency will want a deposit or they'll cancel the reservation.
>
> —A

Great. No pressure there.

She closed out her email, opened up the search page and typed in "St. Celine Island." Several results popped up instantly. She clicked on one of the travel websites and a page of reviews loaded onto her screen:

★ ★ ★ ★ ★ *Best vacation I've ever had.*

The beach was so quiet it felt like we were the only people in the world.

Everyone was so friendly in Ben Harbour. It was like going back to my old hometown.

Beautiful! Easily worth the hour-long boat ride from Nassau.

She clicked on image results and stared at the stunning photographs. Some of the pictures looked professional, but many appeared to be personal images from individuals' blogs and Flickr accounts. There was no doubt as to the serenity and beauty of St. Celine. One of the photos showed a young couple in hiking gear, kissing passionately in front of a gorgeous water-fall, and jealousy stabbed Sarah's chest. She clicked on it.

A blog for someone named Emily84 popped up. The photo was there, along with several others, each more exquisite than the last. She scanned the post. Emily and her husband Josh had apparently honey-mooned on St. Celine, and she gave a moment-by-moment account of their activities of the day spent hik-ing up to the waterfall, a place called La Tour. She detailed everything, including what happened when they got back to Room 202 at the St. Celine Inn. Sa-rah's face was hot by the time she was halfway through, and she wasn't sure if it was from the wine or Emily's descriptions of what she and Josh had done in their bed.

Sarah scrolled down to the bottom of the blog entry. There was a video link. Before she could stop herself she clicked it and was taken to YouTube. It was Emi-ly84's account. The video began to load, and Sarah wondered if she'd stumbled onto the couple's private homemade porn stash. But it was nothing like that. The screen blazed with shots of the deserted beach at the St. Celine Inn. Footage of a young attractive man, dark-bearded and shirtless – presumably Josh – cavort-ing in the downpour of the waterfall from the photographs. He wore a leather necklace with a silver shark's tooth pendant that dangled below the hollow of this throat. "Come on in," he said to the camera. "Put that thing down and get in the water, it's great!" The scene shifted to another shot of a beach, this time taken from a boat. She could hear the thrum of the engine and the crackle of the wind in the microphone. The camera panned over and showed a young woman – Emily – her brown hair tied into a ponytail that looped out of the back of a blue baseball cap, leaning over the white metal railing of the boat, watching the scenery float by. She wore tight red shorts and a bikini top. "There's where we were yesterday," Josh's voice said. His hand appeared in the frame, pointing to a clearing in the trees onshore. The camera zoomed in and focused on the waterfall, partially obscured by its own mist. "It's beautiful," Emily said. The video ended, and Sarah's screen filled with images of other video selections tagged "St. Celine."

She leaned back on the bar stool and took a sip of her wine. What an awesome place. Robert would have loved it. Emily and Josh certainly had. She giggled and wondered what her prim Catholic mother would think reading Emily's explicit accounts of her and Josh's lovemaking.

Well, the decision was made. She was in. Damn all the work she thought she needed to do. It wasn't anything that couldn't wait a couple of weeks. She needed this. If nothing else, she needed it to help herself heal from Robert's death and move forward with her life.

She had just started to close out her browser when something caught her eye. One of the suggested videos on the screen. *Zombie Ritual on St. Celine.* She clicked on it.

The fuzzy video loaded quickly and appeared to have been shot with a cellphone. Something obscured the lens from time to time, and Sarah wondered if the phone had been concealed to shoot this in secret. It showed a raging bonfire in a clearing, then panned over to a group of dark-skinned men and women, dancing rhythmically to the beat of driving drums. Some appeared to be in ritualistic costumes. Others wore street clothes. At their feet lay the still form of a young girl. The drums beat on. The dancers chanted and sang. She'd seen videos and films of vodou rituals from Haiti over the years, and this ceremony appeared similar to those. A woman, perhaps the child's mother, squatted beside the body, her hands uplifted in an imploring motion, and chanted along with the group.

Then a man stepped in from among the dancing participants. He was clad only in white shorts. His chiseled muscular torso was slathered with white paint, and his face was hidden by a large wooden mask with a red skull painted on it. He was obviously a priest of some kind. He was carrying a live chicken by its feet. He squatted and brushed the bird over the girl's body, making the shape of a cross. The drums continued to beat relentlessly and the tempo increased. The ghostly figure in the mask danced faster and wilder, his limbs seemingly unattached from his body. Suddenly he grabbed the chicken by the head and swung its body around in a circle. The bird's wings flapped violently. The priest produced a large dagger and plunged it into the chicken's breast. Blood spurted onto the girl lying prone on the ground, and the man knelt and began drawing symbols on her abdomen with his fingertips.

The drums and chanting stopped. The camera zoomed in on the body on the ground and focused on the girl's face. There was silence for a few long moments.

Suddenly her eyes flew open, and the woman beside her erupted with a scream of joy. She helped the girl sit up, then hugged her tight. The drums and chanting and dancing began again. The girl looked about her, seemingly in a daze.

There was loud commotion off-camera, and then a dark-skinned man came into view, talking harshly to whoever was holding the cellphone. The screen went black and the video ended.

Sarah sat stunned for a moment, still staring at her computer screen. She had no idea if what she had seen was real, a prank or something staged for tourists. But judging by the way the video ended it was not meant to be recorded. She looked at the account that had posted it. *Emily84.* Was that possible?

She clicked on Emily's username and was taken to her gallery of posted videos. "Zombie Ritual on St. Celine" seemed to be the last one uploaded. The date on it was February 23 two years ago.

She paged back through her browser history until she came to Emily's blog. She clicked on the archived list of entries. Emily had been updating her blog and uploading video daily while on her honeymoon. The entry from February 17 began:

> *I'll write my update on yesterday's shenanigans while Josh is still snoring in bed. We stayed up late last night. Again. :)*

The last entry on the blog was dated February 23, the date of the video on YouTube. She skimmed through the words, ignoring the descriptions of the beach and lovemaking in the sand until she got to the last paragraph:

> *Just heard Josh stirring around. I think he may be ready for breakfast, if you know what I mean. :) He's got a surprise for me tonight. We're going to a part of the island tourists don't normally get to see. Not sure how he managed to do that. I'll try to get*

some video. It should be interesting.

That was it. There was nothing more. What had happened? She had evidently returned to the inn and uploaded the video she took with her cellphone. But why no more updates, especially one describing what they had seen?

Sarah scrolled down a bit farther to the comments section. There were fifteen. The first, from Beatleluvr, read *Glad you guys are having a good time. Does Josh know you're writing all this shit about him?*

Gannymeade wrote *How'd you get all the sand out of your hoohah, Em? LOL*

Sarah couldn't help but smile at that. She scrolled down a bit farther until she reached a comment from Nicole0623. She read through it. Then read it again.

> *What's going on? You haven't updated your blog in a couple of days. I found the video you posted on YouTube. WTF is that all about?*

The date on the comment was February 25. Below that was another comment from Nicole0623, this one on February 27:

> *OK, so I guess you guys are "busy" which is why you haven't been writing, but is it too much to ask to let me know everything's OK? There hasn't been anything else on YouTube or even your Facebook page. Did Josh finally get wise to all the nitty gritty you were posting? Haha.*

Then, the last comment on the page. It was dated March 7.

Nicole0623:
For God's sake, Em, where are you two?

Your mom's worrying herself sick after you didn't show up on your flight. Why aren't you answering your phone? I don't know if you're reading these comments or not, but if you see this, please call me or your mom ASAP. Josh's parents have already been in touch with the police.

Sarah continued to stare at the comment. Her stomach burned.

For God's sake, Em.

She drained the rest of her wine and clicked on Emily's blogger profile. The photo was of the girl in the boat video, her hair tucked beneath the same blue baseball cap. She was smiling into the camera. Her face was thin and athletic-looking. Behind her was an expansive mountain range. *Emily84.* Her profile indicated she was from Vancouver and she liked traveling and hiking.

What had happened to her? To them?

Sarah opened another search window and entered "Emily Josh Vancouver." A dozen news stories popped up. She opened the first one.

Still No Clues in Search for Couple

There are still no clues in the disappearance of a Vancouver couple who went missing during their honeymoon on St. Celine in the Bahamas. 24-year-old Josh White and his wife Emily, 22, have not been heard from since February when Emily wrote on her blog that the couple was "going to a part of the island tourists don't normally get to see." An examination of a video of a supposed "zombie ritual" posted on YouTube by Emily White failed to shed any new light on what may have happened to the couple.   A spokesman for the St. Celine Inn where the Whites were staying said the couple's belongings were gone from the room, but they never officially checked out of the hotel.

Authorities on the tiny island of St. Celine have been hampered in their search by the unusually wet rainy season and local flooding. "Everything seems to indicate Mr. and Mrs. White left St. Celine," an official with the Central Detective Unit said, but added his department was cooperating in every way possible with the Royal Canadian Mounted Police.

Sarah clicked back to the search results and found a story from just last month. Her throat tightened as she read it.

Search Ends for Vancouver Couple in Bahamas

Authorities confirmed today that the search has been suspended for Josh and Emily White who went missing on their honeymoon on St. Celine Island in the Bahamas two years ago. Officials declined to provide details but said that exhaustive efforts by local police and volunteers failed to turn up any clues as to what happened to the couple.

"St. Celine is very small and we have searched every inch of it," said Dewayne Munroe, head of the Central Detective Unit in Ben Harbour, the only town on the ten-square-mile island. "Our belief is that the gentleman and his wife left for Canada and something happened to them on their way there."

A spokesperson for the family, Nicole Baker, stated "For everyone who loves Josh and Emily, this is an unfortunate decision. We know they never made it back to Vancouver. They would never just walk away from family and friends. That's not the kind of people they are."

The news article was accompanied by a photograph of Josh and Emily that Sarah recognized from the blog. It had been taken on a boat – the same boat in the video. The two of them stood hugged together, Josh's arm tight around Emily's shoulders, both of them smiling broadly in the bright tropical sun. Josh wore cargo shorts and sunglasses but no shirt. Emily was wearing the outfit from the video. The image blurred and Sarah realized she was blinking back tears.

What could have happened to them? There had to be more information on the case than what she had read. But after twenty minutes of searching news sites and being directed back to the same stories over and over, she gave up. Surely the island's police and the Canadian authorities had combed through everything. But then maybe not. She remembered the Natalie Holloway case, how that stretched for years with no real closure. But that was in Aruba, not on St. Celine.

In any event, she could not stop thinking about the video of the ritual. The last bit of data Emily had uploaded before they disappeared. From an anthropologist's standpoint it was fascinating, all the more so if it were real. She had always heard about such ceremonies, had seen films and videos of them, but had never experienced them firsthand. Maybe if she went to St. Celine there was a chance she could observe one in person.

But without knowing what had happened to Josh and Emily, did she really think that was such a good idea?

Nonsense. Josh and Emily must have fallen in with the wrong people. Perhaps a drug deal gone bad. But she had seen nothing in Emily's blog posts that pointed to drug use. Maybe their libidos had led them down an even darker path, one that had nothing to do with vodou rituals or illegal substances. She and Robert had been warned about such things when they were planning their trip to Cozumel. There was a depraved element in all those tropical vacation spots, and she was sure St. Celine was no exception.

She opened her email and hit reply on Amy's message. *I'm in*, she typed. *Make the call. I'll pay you my half of the deposit tomorrow.* She hit send before she could think any more about it, then shut down the laptop.

Big band music still blared from the TV. It was a slow song by one of the crooners – not Frank or Bing, but someone else. Dick Powell, maybe. She turned it off on her way through the living room.

It was late. What she needed right now was a slow soak in a hot bath and the comfort of her cotton gown.

But once in bed she found herself unable to sleep. She thought the bath and one of Dr. Flores' pills would have been enough to relax her, but she lay for half an hour staring at the ceiling fan before flopping over on her stomach and staring instead into the dark nothingness.

Each time she shut her eyes the vision of the white-painted priest swam before her, dancing and twirling, the eyes in the mask black and dead. She searched her memory for anything she could recall about vodou spirits, but none she remembered had the hideous appearance of the figure in the video. There was Baron Samedi, of course, the god of the dead, but he was usually depicted in these rituals in an almost cartoon fashion – wearing a tuxedo and top hat, swearing and telling filthy jokes. She had seen none of that in the video. This character, or *loa* as they were called, seemed cruel and frightening. She would have to do some research tomorrow when she had some free time.

She had just begun to drift off, had just started floating into blessed sleep, when she heard movement in the room, a slight rustling, like someone shifting on their feet.

Her eyes popped open, straining to see in the blackness. She still lay on her stomach facing the wall. Whatever had made the noise was behind her. Her heart pounded in her ears. She was frozen on the bed.

She thought of the horrible vision of Robert in the attic. Robert sitting in the rocking chair, his dead eyes wide open and locked on her. Her heart was hammering so violently now she could feel the bed shaking with each beat.

There's nothing there! It's your imagination!

But she could feel it. Something was watching her. Its eyes were boring into her. If only she'd let Robert purchase the handgun he'd wanted last summer. "For protection," he'd told her.

But what good was a gun against a ghost? Especially one that only existed in your head?

She took a long, deep breath. It was all that time on the internet tonight. All those stories about Josh and Emily. The disturbing video. It was too much. Her mind was like a rocket sled, blazing along and threatening to fly off the rails.

She whirled over and sat up in the bed, staring toward the doorway. A shape loomed there. Robert? The costumed man from the video?

She reached blindly for the lamp on the bedside table, knocking it over but flooding the room with precious light.

It was her robe, hanging from its hook on the back of the door.

She set the lamp upright and started to switch it off, then changed her mind. Tonight she would probably sleep better if she weren't suffocated by the dark.

She lay back and watched the whirling fan blades until she began to feel dizzy, then closed her eyes. She really was going crazy. Just two more weeks and the semester would be over.   Then she and Amy would take their trip, and she could clear her head. She was glad she had decided to go. It would be exactly what she needed.

8

When Amy read Sarah's response, she actually jumped out of her seat with joy. Yes! She immediately called the travel agent and gave him her credit card number. "It's a go," she told him. "I really appreciate your holding everything for us while my friend decided what she wanted to do."

"Not a problem," the agent said. "If she hadn't said yes, I might have gone instead."

She gave a humorless chuckle. Was he trying to flirt with her? If so, it had just come off as creepy. "You'll email me all the details, right?"

"Going out right now. You girls have fun."

They would fly out of Springfield, change planes in Orlando, and land in Nassau. A shuttle would be waiting to take them to the harbor, where they would board a ferry bound for Ben Harbour. At the island, they had reservations for seven days at the St. Celine Inn. Seven glorious days in paradise, free to lounge on the beach or explore the island at their whim. No students. No classes. No exams to grade, no term papers to read. And for Sarah, no brooding by herself in a creepy old house. It could not be more perfect.

Sarah told her about the couple that had disappeared, and the story was troubling enough that Amy herself had second thoughts about going. But after a bit of searching on the internet she decided it had been an isolated incident. There were no similar stories about St. Celine to be found anywhere, and Amy concluded that the police had been correct. The Whites must have left the island at some point. And she would bet money Vancouver was a hell of a lot more dangerous than Ben Harbour.

The next two weeks were a whirlwind of wrapping up classes, finals and getting grades put into the college's records system. Sarah seemed to have perked up, and Amy was relieved to see traces of the old Sarah shining through. The weekend before their trip, the two of them went shopping for new swimsuits. She chose the skimpiest one she could find; she knew her body wasn't perfect, but if St. Celine's beaches were as sparse as she'd been led to believe, it wouldn't matter. No one would see them anyway, and she wanted to feel sexy. She wasn't surprised when Sarah picked out a modest one-piece; she claimed she wanted all the protection from the tropical sun she could get, but Amy knew better. And it was okay. Sarah was still Sarah.

As their flight left the ground in Springfield, Sarah reached over and squeezed Amy's hand, giving her a big smile. "Thank you for talking me into this," she said.

"You're welcome," Amy told her. "We're gonna have a great time."

9

It was the mornings that made David glad he had come to the island. From the moment the first golden light entered his tiny bedroom until the heat of the day drove him to shade and a cold drink, he knew this was what he had longed for back in Indianapolis. In those winter months when the sun shone brightly but its warmth couldn't penetrate down to where the cold gnawed at his bones. And in the summer, when the heavy humid air smothered the city without so much as a tepid breeze to ease the monotony of the relentless heat rising off the downtown pavement. This was what life was all about. This was worth leaving everything behind in Indiana. Including Beth.

He stretched beneath the sheets, feeling the tired ache in his muscles from the good cleaning he'd given the boat the day before. He washed it at least every other week, more often if he had to clean up after a seasick passenger. He ran a good business, and he wanted everything to look nice and shiny for his customers.

After today he was taking a week off. The spring breakers were gone, and the summer crowds were always lighter; no one wanted a trip to the Bahamas in the middle of the summer. It would be that way until September, when everything would pick up again. Right now he looked forward to lounging around for a bit, maybe heading over to Nassau for a day. It was great being in business for himself, being able to set his own hours and schedule.

He felt weight on his stomach and opened his eyes to see Seymour lying there, watching him with expectant green eyes and twitching whiskers. He and the cat tolerated each other. David provided food and shelter and Seymour kept the house free from lizards and mice. It was a nice arrangement. He reached down and stroked the cat's shaggy gray fur and was rewarded with a loud purr. "Time for breakfast then, huh?" Seymour rubbed his face against David's fingers. "All right, then."

He slipped from the bed and pulled a pair of clean shorts from the dresser drawer, then padded through the house into the kitchen. He filled Seymour's empty bowl, and set about grinding his coffee beans. He loved the coffee here. This was a special blend he bought from a shop in Nassau. It was rich and bold and outrageously expensive, and he'd become addicted to it right after he'd moved to St. Celine. There were a few things worth the extra bucks; his Bahamian-blend coffee and imported Heineken beer were just two of them.

While the coffee brewed, David booted up the laptop and turned on the radio to the station from Freeport; it played a mix of reggae and classic rock, and was what he usually tuned to on his boat. The clientele loved it, and he had to admit it lent a special air to the excursions around the island.

He opened his email and watched the messages slowly fill his inbox. God, the internet was slow here, when it worked at all, and he wondered often if the term "high-speed" meant something different down here in the islands. There were a couple of items from his website, bookings for the middle of June from the automatic scheduler he had set up, and nice fat payments from PayPal to accompany them. In the two years he had been running Burke's Island Tours he had seen the business grow by word-of-mouth from one or two bookings a week to a full schedule of three a day. He had set up the automatic booking site because it had become impossible for him to schedule tours by phone. Now he simply let the internet do the work for him, and all he had to do was show up and captain the boat. It was a perfect arrangement.

There was a message from his mother, and he felt a stab of panic until he realized it was just another of her guilt-inducing notes begging him to call more often or come home for a visit. She was good at pulling irritation out of him, even if all she did was send a message saying "Hi." It was almost as if he could hear her voice, tinged with sadness and self-pity, trying to shame him for his decision to pack up and leave Indianapolis. "Your father says hello," she wrote today. "I'm sure he'd like to hear from you, too."

Not bloody likely.

When he had told his parents he was leaving his high-paying and extremely stressful job in the investment department at the bank to move to the Bahamas, they both looked at him like he had drowned a sack full of kittens. His dad took it especially hard. "Why in the name of God would you want to do that?"

"Because the pressure is killing me," David told him. He almost told them about the panic attacks that had been dogging him for a couple of months – episodes where he wondered if his heart was about to beat through his chest and leave him lifeless in his suit and tie behind the desk in his windowless office on the ninth floor – but he figured it would just worry his mother even more. "I've got to make some changes."

His father's eyes narrowed. "How are you gonna support yourself down there? It won't be a permanent vacation, you know. You'll have to work."

"I've got my investments," David said.

"You mean your retirement funds."

"Yep. It's enough to get me set up and have some left over. I've bought a house there on a little island called St. Celine. You two would love it there. And I've bought a boat."

His father blew out a breath. "A boat."

"It's actually a business," David said. "A going concern. Harbor cruises." He didn't tell them the boat was an ancient rusting power catamaran, held together mostly with duct tape and baling wire, and that the "going concern" consisted mostly of picking up the overflow from another more successful tour boat. But it was his. And he knew he could make a go of it. He just knew it.

"I think you're a damned fool," his father said. "Leaving a great job to go down there and be nothing but a beach bum. You'll be bankrupt in a year. Your brother would never do anything this stupid."

Of course not. Kevin was the perfect child. Sickening as little brothers went. Like David, he had pursued a career in banking. But Kevin had thrived on the atmosphere of greed and power plays that David found to be a passionless soul suck. Now he headed up a large regional holding company in Atlanta – the youngest CEO ever for that organization. He'd even made the cover of *American Banker* magazine, which their parents proudly displayed in a frame on their wall.

His mother was more subtle, but she knew which buttons to push. "What does Beth think about it?"

And that was the only part of the plan that gave him pause. Beth was not happy about it. Not at all. She had her heart set on marrying David the wealthy banker, of throwing swanky parties and upscale barbecues at their big house on the north end of the city and sending their kids to private schools. She certainly didn't envision herself working and sweating in the tropical sun, not unless there was a handsome cabana boy to bring her a piña colada on an hourly basis. And the idea of abandoning Indianapolis society and its prestige after all the years her parents had worked to establish their position was almost more than she could bear. But at the moment all he could think to say was something to get his parents off his back. "She'll come around," he told them.

But she hadn't. In the end their parting was painful. And while he knew what he was doing was necessary to keep himself out of an early grave, that thought did little to console him on those lonely nights in an empty bed. That first year he thought often that maybe he should have tried harder to persuade Beth to join him, and that if she had only spent a few weeks here she would have suddenly changed her mind. But he knew that was impossible. Beth would never have embraced the island lifestyle. Her coming here would have only delayed the inevitable. It was best that she had stayed in Indy. Best they had parted swiftly and cleanly.

He closed out his email and logged into his investment accounts. He had switched some funds around a few weeks ago, and he was pleased to see his gut instinct had been correct. Overall his accounts were up seven percent since the realignment. It was good to know he still had it. The interest off his accounts combined with the income from the tour boat was enough to keep him comfortable in this new scaled-back life he had claimed. He allowed himself a few luxuries, like the coffee he was now sipping and the red Honda Shadow that sat in his gravel driveway, but for the most part he prided himself on his ability to live frugally and simply.

It was that innate thriftiness that had allowed him a few months ago to pay cash for a newer used catamaran, the *New Beginning*. It was a beautiful boat, with a shaded lounge area that could hold twenty people, a small sun deck, and a premium sound system. The *New Beginning* made his old boat, the *Keylypso*, seem like a derelict piece of garbage suitable only for scrap. He had bought it from a retired couple on the island; they had come down from Atlanta to spend their golden years, but decided after a few months that the lifestyle was not for them and returned to the States. The boat had barely been used, but the couple was desperate to sell it, and David got an exceptional deal.

He slid open the door to the deck, stepped over Seymour as he slipped between his feet, and settled into a chair overlooking the forest behind the house. Tall, spindly Bahamian pines sprouted from a shrubby dense undergrowth of palmettos and ferns. And while he couldn't see the water from his place, the soundtrack of birds and insects in the surrounding vegetation was more than enough to create a relaxing environment to enjoy the morning. The hot coffee in his stomach combined with the early sunlight warming his bare chest gave him such intense physical pleasure that he knew beyond any doubt he had been destined for this place. Indianapolis and all its trappings were far away, a world so different from this that at times it felt like the last vestiges of a dream he could shake from his head and forget. It was these moments when he knew he had made the right decision to leave everything behind.

His cup drained, he stood and stretched, noticing as he did so how much his belly had grown since coming here. Back in Indy he had made an effort to visit the gym at least three times a week, huffing on the treadmill or hitting the weights. But on St. Celine there were no gyms. Moreover, there was no reason for working out. He wasn't out to impress anyone. He ate healthy, even if he tended to overindulge sometimes, and he stayed active with his work. He supposed now that he was in his thirties, relaxing more and stressing a lot less, he simply wasn't burning the calories he used to. Well, that and too many margaritas down at Jolly Roger's.

Back in the house, he grabbed a shirt, stepped into his shoes and headed out for town on the Honda. His road wasn't paved, and some days it felt like he was riding a dirt bike through the woods. The heavy rains in the early spring had left new ruts across the low spots, and it would probably be August before a road crew came around to fill them in and smooth out the road. If then. No one got in a hurry on St. Celine.

Though it was early, a few tourists were already out in Ben Harbour, cruising up and down the main thoroughfare on rented golf carts or strolling along the sidewalks sipping coffee from the shop on the corner. A lot of the oldtimers on the island hated tourists. They complained about the messes they left or how rude they were or how much congestion they caused on the streets. But he knew these same complainers were always more than happy to take their money. David was always happy to see them. There were the occasional drunken idiots or the families with unruly brats, but most everyone was friendly and easygoing.

He parked the Honda at the dock next to the office and waved at Jimmy through the window as he passed. Jimmy gave him a wide-toothed grin and threw up his hand. David never had to worry about leaving his bike here. Not only did Jimmy keep a good eye on things, but crime was just nearly unheard of on the island. Except for the intermittent domestic dispute or brawls usually instigated by intoxicated visitors, the police on St. Celine had it pretty easy.

Gulls swooped down over the docks, screeching at each other and riding the breezes around the moored vessels. The harbor was fairly small. Many of the boats that made their home here were fishing vessels; a lot of men on the island made their living selling their catch to the local restaurants and markets, and most of them were already out for the day. The ferry dock was full of people waiting to make the return trip to Nassau. They were overnight guests, towing suitcases and luggage. Just off the dock, the cabs and hotel vans were lining up to catch the next batch. The 8:45 ferry would also bring in the early batch of daytrippers – some from the big island resorts, some on excursions from the cruise ships that docked for the day in Nassau harbor. These were the guests that were his bread and butter, the ones with big money to spend, the ones who had booked their island tour weeks or months in advance.

Next to the *New Beginning* was a large Hatteras Express fishing boat, the *Sundancer*. Its owner, Eric Durand, made a fortune chartering deep sea fishing trips, mostly from businessmen who fantasized about hooking a marlin or a sailfish and were willing to plunk down a thousand bucks a day for the chance. Eric was a native to the island – born and raised here. He'd been a big help getting David set up and established and was a good friend. This morning he sat perched atop the handrails at the top of the gangplank that led up to the back of the boat, swinging his lanky khaki-clad legs to the beat of the reggae music he was blasting over the boat's sound system. "What up?" he called.

David stopped at the foot of the gangplank. "Oh, you know, the usual." He swiped a hand across his scruffy face. He needed to shave, but he rarely did. "Got a full day?"

Eric swung his sunglasses to the top of his head. "Two trips today, morning and afternoon. Big group for the afternoon. They requested lots of beverages."

David laughed. Eric sold beer on his boat, mostly Budweiser, though he also kept a good supply of Kalik and Red Stripe to provide an authentic island experience. At six bucks a pop he earned a tidy profit, especially on days when no one was catching anything. David didn't supply any refreshments other than a cooler full of free bottled water; it was too much work stocking drinks, and if he was piloting the boat he couldn't operate a snack bar. And he damn sure didn't want to hire any extra help. "I got three full loads today myself," he said. "Big troup of British gents for my two o'clock." He dreaded it; people from the U.K. wilted in the tropical heat and tended to complain about it.

Eric grinned. "Serving tea and crumpets?" he said,

raising an imaginary cup and extending a pinkie.

Eric had the usual island accent, though he exaggerated it for tourists, and hearing him try to sound like an Englishman was just too much. "Been smoking weed already today, dude?"

"I tell you I get the best. You have to join me in a toke one of these days."

David shook his head and laughed. Eric was far from being a stoner – he was a devout Catholic and dedicated to his wife and two kids – but they joked about it all the time. They were both asked at least twice a week by tourists where to make a score. It was mostly wealthy college kids or affluent young couples, but once in a while some of the older folks would inquire as well. David knew it was available in Nassau, but in the two years he had been in Ben Harbour he had yet to even see a joint. That kind of stuff just didn't go on here.

Across the dock, David could see the ferry making its way through the turquoise water of the harbor. "Ferry's early today."

Eric turned his dark face toward the dock and stroked the black wispy whiskers on his chin. "Something's up," he said.

"What do you mean?"

Eric popped his sunglasses back on his face and continued to watch the ferry move closer. "I don't know. But something is in the air, my friend. There is a change coming." He hopped off the handrails and moved toward the front of the boat, leaving David rooted at the foot of the gangplank.

II

ST. CELINE

E ven as much as she had traveled, Sarah was still excited every time she touched down in a new location. Today was no exception.

Though their flight from Orlando was delayed by half an hour, they had no problem finding a waiting shuttle to take them to the harbor to catch the ferry. Topping the bridge and seeing the monstrous cruise ships docked for the day in that bright blue water filled her with a sudden elation she hadn't expected. It was as though something in her had awakened, some deep part of her that had been dormant and shuttered since Robert had died.

Amy pointed across the harbor beyond the ships. "There's Atlantis," she said.

Sarah squinted at the spires rising through the haze. "Ever stayed there?"

Amy shook her head. "Tim and I talked about it, but we never came. I've seen the commercials on TV. It looks fabulous."

The shuttle driver, an older dark-skinned gentleman with curly white hair peeking from beneath his black cap, caught Sarah's eye in the rearview mirror. "Where you ladies going?"

"St. Celine," Amy said.

"Ah," he said. "Glad I asked. I take you straight to the ferry dock." He winked at Sarah and she felt her face flush. "I know a shortcut."

Just across the bridge he took a sharp right down a narrow tree-lined street. Cars and vans choked the avenue, and horns blared from all directions. Sarah held her breath as the shuttle inched closer and closer to the black sedan ahead of them.

"Don't be nervous," said the driver. "I need only two inches of clearance. Just two inches."

Vehicles merged from out of nowhere as they crept down the street. The cars going the other direction looked as if they would scrape the side of the shuttle at any moment, but they passed with just millimeters to spare.

"See?" the driver said. "Two inches."

Amy leaned in closer to Sarah. "I bet two inches is all he's got," she whispered. She giggled and poked Sarah in the ribs.

Sarah tried to keep a straight face. The driver was studying her in the mirror. But she couldn't hold it any longer, and she erupted with laughter. Then Amy was laughing, too. They giggled and rolled around in the seat of the shuttle like two drunken fools. Sarah clutched Amy's arm as the shuttle flew around a sharp bend, and they howled. There were tears in Sarah's eyes and her stomach spasmed with the force of her laughter. She gasped for breath. She hadn't felt this good in months. It was wonderful.

At the dock, the shuttle stopped at the gate and the driver helped them unload their bags. "I am sure you ladies will have a great time. St. Celine is a beautiful place. But stay close to Ben Harbour and the beaches."

Sarah looked at him. "What do you mean?"

The driver kept his gaze on their luggage. "The rest of the island is wild. Untamed. Dangerous if you don't know where you're going. Best to stay close to where other people are."

Amy locked glances with Sarah, then pressed a five dollar bill into the man's hand. "Well, thank you for getting us here."

The man smiled and bowed slightly. "It was my pleasure."

As he drove away, Amy stared after him. "What the hell do you make of that?"

Sarah shook her head. "Weird."

Amy shrugged and pulled her suitcase toward the gate. "Well, let's forget it. I think he was checking you out, anyway."

"Stop it."

"No, really. I saw him looking at your ass when you were getting out of the shuttle."

"He was not looking at my ass."

Amy laughed. "Yes, he was, I swear."

"No one looks at my ass."

"Whatever. You might have just missed your chance for a holiday fling."

Sarah swatted her. "He's probably got a wife and ten kids at home."

"And fifteen grandchildren," Amy said.

"Well," Sarah said, "he can certainly do a lot with his two inches."

2

The ferry ride out of the harbor was quiet and pleasant. A breeze fanned them where they sat at the front of the boat, and the sun was warm but not hot enough to be uncomfortable.

Amy gazed at the mansions slipping by on the shore, wondering what these people could do that afforded such luxury. Many of them had their own boat slips with glistening yachts moored at the water's edge. Behind the homes on the harbor front other houses clung to the hillside beyond, no doubt offering spectacular views of the water and the city of Nassau on the other side.

She had never seen water this color before – a blue that matched the turquoise jewelry she had purchased in Arizona when she was a girl. It was almost unreal, like some Hollywood special effect. It certainly wasn't the muddy brown of the lakes and rivers she had grown up around in Texas.

She looked at Sarah, sitting beside her with her hands folded in her lap. "It's beautiful, isn't it?"

"It really is," Sarah said, not looking at her. She opened her mouth to say something else, then closed it.

"What?"

"I keep thinking about Josh and Emily."

"Who?"

"The couple that disappeared. And what the driver said, about staying close to the town and other people."

"Look, Sarah, don't let that old man spook you."

"Well what do you think he meant?"

Amy stared ahead at the sunlight glistening on the water. "Who knows."

"Emily's last blog entry talked about going somewhere tourists didn't normally see."

Amy clenched her jaw. "Will you stop dwelling on that?"

"But you saw the video."

Amy took a deep breath. "Yes, I saw it. The police saw it, too, and I'm sure they investigated it."

"The point is," Sarah said, "Josh and Emily obviously went somewhere away from the safe parts of the island. Somewhere they weren't supposed to go."

"So we won't go anywhere we're not supposed to," Amy said. "We'll stay on the beach. We won't leave the town. We'll be fine." She put her hand on Sarah's arm. "Don't freak out on me, girl."

Sarah smiled and hung her head. "Sorry, I just get..."

"Carried away?" Amy said.

Sarah laughed. "Do I?"

Amy nodded. "Little bit."

When the ferry docked at Ben Harbour, a van was waiting to take them to the inn. Marko, the driver, was younger than the shuttle driver in Nassau and not as friendly and talkative. But he handled their bags with swift precision, which suited Amy fine. Efficiency was worth more than small talk any day.

The main street through Ben Harbour was lined with shops painted a variety of pastel colors and offering everything from rum cakes to hair braiding, much of the same thing they had seen in the airport in Nassau. Tourists, most of them looking like they had stepped out of an Old Navy commercial, wandered the side- walks lugging shopping bags and carrying drinks. And while the small portion of Nassau they had encountered was dingy and dusty, Ben Harbour was fresh and pris- tine as Disneyland.

"Our shuttle makes regular trips between the inn and town," Marko said. "It runs from nine in the morning until midnight."

Golf carts were everywhere, and seemed to be the vehicle of choice for visitors choosing not to walk. "Can you rent the carts somewhere?" Amy asked.

"Several places in town," he said. "The inn has them as well. Rent them by the day or for your whole stay. You want to reserve one early. They are very popular."

"That would be fun," Sarah said.

"It is a great way to see the island on your own," he said.

"Can we take a golf cart to the big waterfall?" Amy asked.

Marko looked over his shoulder at her. "You mean La Tour?" He shook his head. "You will have to hike from the inn to reach La Tour."

"Is it far?" Sarah asked.

Marko laughed. "Nothing is far on St. Celine."

The wide street narrowed as they rounded a bend and

the shops gave way to palm and pine forest. The van climbed a small slope and the inn came into view, a row of two-story colonial style houses with wide front porches and railed balconies. Brightly colored, lush clusters of red, yellow, and purple bushes dotted the landscape amid towering palm trees and shrub-like ferns. A stone fountain guarded the main entrance, and several tiny birds splashed about in its uppermost tier. Amy couldn't imagine the big resorts at Nassau having this much charm and character.

Marko pulled around the fountain and stopped at the double doors of the main building. "Welcome to the St. Celine Inn," he said.

Two bellmen immediately opened the back hatch and began unloading the luggage onto a cart. "Welcome, ladies," one of them said. "I trust you had a pleasant journey."

"Yes, thanks," Amy said.

"It's beautiful here," Sarah said, pulling off her sunglasses. "I'm sure you get tired of people saying that."

"It never gets old," the other bellman said. "We are very proud of our inn."

The beauty inside rivaled that of the gardens, with a marble-tiled floor and furnishings of rich mahogany wood. Ceiling fans hung from the exposed beam ceiling, whirling lazily in the afternoon heat. Light filtered in through the high transom windows that encircled the lobby. Groupings of plush chairs and settees were scattered throughout, divided by large potted palms.

The clerk at the front desk, with skin the color of dark chocolate and her black hair pulled into neat plaits, greeted them with an open-mouthed smile. "May I help you, ladies?"

"Reservation for Vandiver," Amy said.

"Ah, yes, Miss Vandiver," the clerk said.   She checked the computer monitor in front of her. "With us for seven nights?"

"Correct."

The clerk slid two key cards across the counter. "You're all set.   Second floor of Building One with a private verandah overlooking the water."

"Sounds like heaven," Amy said.

The clerk's bright red lips curled into an easy smile. "As close as you're likely to get in this life."

3

Their room was 204, and Sarah felt an eerie unease when she realized it was right next door to the room where Josh and Emily had stayed. She looked at the brass numbers as they passed it, feeling her face flush as she remembered reading Emily's posts about what all had happened in that room. But what else had gone on in there? What happened between the time Emily uploaded the video and they vanished from the inn?

But her thoughts were cut short when Amy unlocked their door and exclaimed, "Holy shit!"

The room was spacious and airy with white sheer curtains outlining a set of French doors that opened onto the private verandah. The two double beds were bedecked with crisp white linens and piled high with fluffy pillows. A ceiling fan hung from the white beadboard ceiling, stirring the ocean air that drifted in through the open windows.

Amy opened the French doors. "Come look out here!"

The verandah overlooked a garden of bougainvillea and hibiscus that stretched toward the tree-lined cliff above the pink-sand beach. Beyond was the turquoise sea, glistening in the brilliant sunlight. Below them, several peacocks roamed freely about the grounds.

Sarah snapped a few pictures with her phone. She was practically giddy with excitement. "I know I keep saying this, but it's so beautiful!"

Amy took a deep breath. "Let's put our things away and hit the beach."

The short walk to the water wound past the sparkling pool, strangely empty at this time of the afternoon, and down a narrow sandy trail carved between two rocky cliffs. Just past a small cluster of palmettos, the path widened and opened onto a sprawling pink beach facing a small bay created by a long breakwater several hundred yards out. Lounge chairs were lined up along the sand, punctuated at intervals with orange umbrellas, and several hammocks swayed where the sand butted up against the forest. Two couples had dragged chairs down to the water's edge, and they sat in a semi-circle, talking and stirring the water with their legs. There was no one else around.

Sarah was glad she had bought the one-piece, even though they were virtually alone down here. Amy's top barely covered her breasts, and Sarah knew she could never feel comfortable in anything that skimpy. Not that she was a prude. But she knew her own limits, whether inspired by her own self-doubt or the sisters at St. Thomas Catholic School all those years ago.

She dug into her bag and pulled out a spray can of

Coppertone. "Sunscreen?" she asked Amy.

Amy was setting her things beside a lounge chair under one of the umbrellas. "Sure."

Sarah took a seat in the shade and stared out at the water. Such an endless vivid blue. The cool breeze coming off the sea smelled of salt. She closed her eyes and let it caress her. The waves here lapped gently at the shore; it wasn't the monotonous crashing she remembered from trips to the Atlantic coast in Florida. This was different. Peaceful. Quiet. A lone gray gull soared over the bay, riding the wind and giving a single cry.

Amy nudged her with the can. "What'cha thinking about?"

Sarah took the can and sprayed her legs. "How glad I am you talked me into this."

"It's great, isn't it? I knew it would be fabulous, but I never expected this." She drew her legs up and hugged them, then took a deep breath. Sarah couldn't see her eyes behind the dark sunglasses, but she imagined they were closed. "I love the sea. Of course I didn't see much of it when Tim and I were on our honeymoon."

Sarah blushed and sprayed sunscreen on her arms. She was pale, almost pasty, from staying indoors, and she knew she would need to be careful to not burn. Amy's complexion was naturally dark, the kind that tanned easily, and Sarah envied her.

"Of course, I haven't traveled nearly as much as you," Amy went on. "Tim and I had lots of plans, but we never followed through with them."

"That's a shame."

"Yeah. It is."

A shadow drifted over her, and Sarah jumped as a

man in a dark jacket appeared at her side. "May I get you ladies something from the bar?" He was carrying a silver tray and wearing white gloves. He seemed so out of place that for a moment Sarah wondered if she was seeing things again.

"Sure," Amy said. "I'll take a strawberry margarita."

Sarah realized he was staring at her, expecting a response. "Oh," she said, "nothing for me, thanks. Except maybe some water. Can I get a bottled water?"

He nodded. "I'll be back shortly."

They watched him trudge away toward the path back to the hotel, and Amy said, "Wow, beachside service. I didn't expect that."

Sarah looked back at the bay and the breakwater beyond. A single lamp post was positioned at the end of it. It leaned slightly to the right, no doubt the victim of years of winds off the ocean. She recognized it from the background in a few of Emily's pictures.

Suddenly, the breeze was cold. Emily and Josh had been here. They had lounged here on the sand just as she and Amy were now. According to Emily's blog, they had made love here. Maybe they had sat on these very chairs. Sarah shivered.

"You okay?" Amy said.

Sarah managed a smile. She had hoped Amy didn't notice. "I'm fine." She didn't want another lecture about not freaking out. "Just got a chill."

"What about going into town later? Look at some of the shops, maybe grab a bite to eat."

Sarah shrugged. "Sure." She had actually looked forward to a nice dinner in the inn, then settling down early in bed with a book. The trip down had worn her out. But there would be plenty of time to rest in the days ahead. Amy was excited to be somewhere new, and Sarah refused to be a killjoy. Besides, this trip was all about creating new memories and having new experiences. It was not about locking herself up in her room for a week and brooding. She refused to do that. Robert would not have wanted that.

The waiter reappeared with their drinks, and Amy signed the charge slip. "You're a cheap date," she told Sarah.

Sarah laughed and cracked open the bottle. She held it out to Amy for a toast. "Here's to new experiences," she said.

Amy tapped her glass against the water bottle. "I'll drink to that."

J ust as the afternoon sun began to dip to the horizon, Amy and Sarah took the shuttle from the inn down the hill to town, where they were dropped off at the end of Main Street. It was similar to all the other tourist traps Amy had seen back home, with cheap souvenirs, overpriced food, and lounges offering karaoke with no cover charge.

Sarah looked beat, and Amy wondered if coming to town tonight had been a good idea. The street was clean but crowded, and she could tell Sarah was not enjoying weaving through the hordes of people. So when they reached a small pub called Jolly Roger's, she took Sarah's arm and pulled her inside. "Let's get something to eat," she said, and Sarah nodded.

The place was dark and loud. Jimmy Buffett was blasting over the sound system and a group of raucous young men had taken over the corner by the pool table. Everyone appeared to be having a good time, and all the tables were full. Amy was just about to suggest they go find someplace else when she spotted two seats at the end of the bar. She motioned to Sarah and they weaved their way through the sea of tables toward the empty corner. "How's this?"

"Works for me." She rubbed her temples.

"You okay?"

Sarah nodded. "I'm just tired."

A young blonde woman appeared beside them instantly. She was wearing a kerchief printed with a skull and crossbones pattern. "What can I get you ladies?"

"What's good?" Amy asked.

"The crab nachos are the best you'll find anywhere."

Amy looked at Sarah. "Help me eat them?"

Sarah nodded. "Sure."

"And I'll take a Bud Light," Amy said.

"Diet Coke," said Sarah.

When the server was gone, Amy leaned closer to Sarah. "You sure you're all right?"

"I'm fine."

Amy was suddenly aware of the man sitting next to her. He was slightly pudgy with closely-cropped reddish-blond hair, scruffy but with a neatly-trimmed goatee. His ruddy complexion and masculine scent hinted that he had been outside most of the day. To some women this might have been a turn-off, repulsive even, but Amy found it strangely enticing. Arousing. He caught her staring and gave her a puzzled smile. His eyes were bright blue and clear. "Oh, sorry," she said.

"The customary word here is 'hello,'" he told her and grinned.

She felt her face grow hot. "Of course. Hello."

"Hi."

She extended her hand and he took it. "I'm Amy."

"David."

She felt a poke in her shoulder and turned to see Sarah glaring at her. "And this is my friend, Sarah."

He nodded. "Hey, Sarah."

Sarah leaned forward, straining to hear above the noise. "What did you say your name was again?"

"David," he said louder. "David Burke."

The waitress brought their drinks and Amy took a sip of her beer. "Where you from?"

"Indianapolis originally."

"And now?"

"I live here on the island."

"Really?"

"Yeah. Couple of years now."

Sarah leaned forward. "So what do you do?"

"I have a tour boat," David said. "Excursions around the island. You know, sightseeing." He swirled his bottle of Heineken. "So what do you ladies do?"

"We're instructors at Cedar Hill State College. You've probably never heard of it."

"Actually, I know where that is," he said. "My brother went there."

Amy gaped at him. "No kidding!"

"That was a few years back." He smiled and took a drink. "What do you teach?"

"I teach sociology," Amy said, "And Sarah – "

"Anthropology," Sarah said. She gave Amy a slight smile.

"Went to Indiana myself," David said. He pumped his fist. "Go Hoosiers."

The waitress returned with their steaming platter of nachos. It smelled heavenly. Amy grabbed a crab and cheese covered chip and sank her teeth into it. It was the best thing she'd had in months. She elbowed David. "Want some?"

"No, thanks," he said. "And I'd go light on those if I were you. Eat too much of that and you'll regret it later."

Amy shoved the rest of the cheesy concoction into her mouth. "I'll keep that in mind." Beside her, Sarah had forked out a portion on a small plate and was daintily trying to pull a single chip out of the pile. "Just eat it, Sarah. Get your fingers in it."

Sarah managed to pull off a corner and deposit it into her mouth. "Mm, that's delicious."

David drained the rest of his beer and set the empty bottle on the bar. "Well, you guys enjoy your vacation."

"You're going already?" Amy said, her mouth full.

He nodded. "Yeah. Been a long day."

"Wait." She grabbed his sleeve. "How do we find you for a tour?"

"Yeah," said Sarah, "that sounds like fun."

David shrugged. "Afraid you're out of luck this week. I'm taking a few days off. How long you going to be here?"

"Just until next Sunday," Amy said, surprised at how disappointed she felt.

David looked at her. A crooked grin crept across his face. "You got any plans for tomorrow?"

Amy glanced at Sarah and they both shook their heads. "No, not really."

David blew out a breath. "Tell you what. Come to the marina tomorrow. My boat's in slip twenty-three. The *New Beginning*. Look for the sign that says 'Burke's Island Tours.' I'll meet you there about ten. I'll give you a free tour."

"You sure?" Amy said. "We don't want to put you to any trouble."

He smiled and gave a shrug. "No trouble. I'd probably be going out there anyway to check on things."

"That's really nice of you," Sarah said. "But we couldn't ask you to do it for free."

He held up his hand. "It's nothing. I'll see you tomorrow." He turned and slipped into the crowd.

Amy looked back at Sarah. "Well. What do you think of that?"

"I hope he's not some kind of creep," Sarah said.

Amy turned back to the bar and dug into the nachos. "He's not a creep." She glanced back to where he had disappeared. "He's kind of cute."

Sarah gaped at her. "Are you kidding? He looks like Larry the Cable Guy."

Amy slapped her on the shoulder. "No, he doesn't!"

Sarah giggled. "He does!"

Amy smiled and took a sip of her beer. David *had* been kind of beefy and disheveled. But she liked that in a guy. Such a far cry from Tim's well-manicured hands and overpriced haircut. David was manly. Brawny. And he had stirred something in her that hearkened back to those early days just after the divorce. Something that smoldered in her. She felt a grin creeping across her face and covered it by shoving more of the crab nachos into her mouth. *It's lust, my dear lady, no doubt about it.* It had been months since she had been with a guy – that flirty dude she'd met in a club back in Cedar Hill, the one she took out to the parking lot and devoured. He had shoved her against the wall of the building and they had gone at it like wild animals right there in the open. She could still feel the bricks against her back, still feel they heat they gave off from soaking up the afternoon sun. Neither of them had lasted long. They were too excited, too liquored up to care about anything but their own needs. She had never seen him again. They didn't even exchange phone numbers.

She took a deep breath of the smoky air, tasted the beer and sweet crab meat on her tongue. She had to be good on this trip. For Sarah. For herself. This was the new Amy. The good girl. The one her old Sunday school teacher would have been proud of.

Beside her, Sarah sipped her Diet Coke through a straw, watching her. "You're still thinking about him, aren't you?"

Amy felt her face flush hot. "Of course I'm still thinking about him. And you're convinced he's a weir-do."

Sarah hoisted a loaded tortilla chip to her mouth. "Well, we don't know anything about him. Some strange guy inviting us to his boat. You're not at least a little bit. . . leery?"

Amy frowned. "I know I should be."

"I'm just being cautious," Sarah said, her mouth full. She swallowed and stared at the mirror behind the wall. "I keep thinking about Josh and Emily."

Amy met Sarah's gaze in the mirror. "If you don't want to go, we don't have to. I just think it would be fun." She picked up her beer, then set it back down. "Tell you what. We'll ask about him at the inn. It's a small island. I'm sure they know who he is." She looked at Sarah and saw her visibly relax. "Would that make you feel better?"

Sarah nodded. "Yes. Thank you."

Amy smiled and took a drink of beer. "Let's finish these nachos and get back to our room. I'm exhausted."

5

David unlocked the front door, flipped on the lights and tossed his keys into the bowl on the cabinet. What in God's name was he thinking, inviting two women onto his boat for a free tour? And during what was supposed to be his vacation?

Seymour looked up from his spot on the couch, blinking lazily in the sudden brightness. He stretched out to his full length, then made his way over to rub against David's legs, purring loudly. David bent down and scratched him behind the ears, feeling the aftereffects of the Jolly Roger's flameburger as he did so. God. He knew he should have taken off half the jalapeños when he saw them.

He pulled out of his shirt and headed toward the bathroom for a quick shower, turning on the lights through the house as he did so. Who was he kidding? He knew why he'd invited them for a free tour. They were hot, both of them. Especially that Amy with her dark hair and soft brown eyes. Eyes that had stayed on him during their brief conversation. And the way she had caught his sleeve when he turned to leave. How could he refuse that?

He started the water and stared at himself in the mirror. Once a long time ago he could have fooled himself into thinking he was fairly nice looking. But that was back when he dressed in Brooks Brothers suits and kept a decent haircut. Tonight he looked like a beached walrus. Probably smelled like one, too.

The steam from the shower fogged up the mirror and he stepped into the tub. What was he doing? He had told himself when he came down here that he wouldn't get involved with anyone, especially a tourist. He hadn't been with anyone since Beth. He wanted to keep it that way. Relationships just complicated things. And wasn't simplifying his life the whole reason for coming to St. Celine?

Still, once he was out of the shower he lathered up his face and gave himself a good shave, then used a pair of barber scissors to trim the stray whiskers popping out of his beard. It was a shame he couldn't do anything about the scattered white hairs that had begun popping up on his chin. Or his head for that matter.

Satisfied that he had made himself as presentable as possible, he pulled on a pair of shorts and grabbed a beer from the refrigerator. Seymour was again splayed out on the couch. "Get up, you lazy thing," David told him. Seymour didn't move. Cats. What good were they, anyway?

Along one wall of the living room were shelves that housed David's vinyl record collection. He'd been collecting since he was a kid, and now he had a couple thousand albums lined up next to his vintage Bang and

Olufsen turntable. He pulled out a John Coltrane record and in a moment sweet, cool jazz filled the house. Getting the albums here had been a real bitch. He'd had them shipped in wooden crates by air to Nassau, then paid a moving company a small fortune to cart them over to the island, terrified all the while that his precious LPs would melt like candle wax in the Bahamian heat. But they survived the trip very well. Over the past couple of years he had added a few to his collection, most from a second-hand store in Freeport. There was something about the sound of vinyl that couldn't be equaled in those sterile emotionless MP3s.

He slipped through the kitchen and out the patio doors to the deck. Even through the canopy of pines, he was always amazed at how clear and bright the stars were here. He leaned back in his chair and gazed at the sky. The Coltrane floated through the air, mixing with the night sounds of the forest. The beer was cold and crisp on his lips, and the soft breeze was cool on his skin. Pleasant as it was, these moments were when he hated living alone. As much as he valued his freedom, this bit of paradise would be so much sweeter if there were someone to share it with. Someone he could hold against him while they both watched the skies. Someone to make love with.

He wondered again about tomorrow, about Amy and Sarah. He was a fool for even considering this would be anything other than a normal excursion around the island. The day would end, the girls would go back to their hotel, and they would never see each other again. Just like his usual customers.

Beth's face flashed before him, and he immediately felt guilty. Why, he didn't know. Even after two years, he couldn't shake the weight of her memory. Especially when he thought of other women. She seemed to still be there. Accusing him, shaming him. And he knew he could never begin another relationship until he had exorcised the last of her out of his system. She always seemed to pop to the forefront of his conscious when, like tonight, he was feeling especially horny.

The Coltrane record ended, and now the night sounds pressed in all around him. Seymour had wandered out onto the deck and was concentrating on a spot between the wooden planks and the siding of the house where small lizards sometimes came and went.

David had just drained the last of his beer when he heard something in the distance. It sounded like. . . *drums*. At first he thought maybe he was catching some noise from Ben Harbour, maybe from one of the clubs. But the sound was coming from the north, through the forest and up the hills, away from town. He stood against the deck railing, his eyes searching the darkness and his ears straining to catch the rhythm. It *was* drums. He had never heard anything like it before, driving and primal. And coming from the part of the island that he'd been told was uninhabited and wild.

Very odd. He'd have to remember to ask Eric about it tomorrow.

6

David had been right about the crab nachos.

Sarah awoke at four with her stomach in knots. She tiptoed to the bathroom in the darkness and sat in misery on the toilet for half an hour. And by the time she was completely emptied out, she was exhausted. She returned to bed but no position she twisted into was comfortable. She lay there, staring at the ceiling and watching the gray light creep into the room and listening to Amy snore. She found her phone and hopped on the inn's wi-fi to check her email, but there was nothing except sales ads for Fab and Macy's. She deleted them, then turned off the phone and watched the ceiling fan for a while. Finally at five-thirty she dragged herself from the bed and slipped out onto the verandah.

The sun had not yet risen, and the eastern sky and the sea were the color of gold. She stood against the balustrade and let the breeze off the water caress her skin; it was chilly but not unpleasant. Below her, the peacocks strolled like ladies in ball gowns, stopping occasionally to peck at the ground.

She settled into one of the white wooden rockers on the verandah, afraid to make any noise and spoil this magic moment. Robert would have loved this place. It was ten times more beautiful than any other Caribbean island she had ever visited. And though she'd never made it to Cozumel after the accident, she couldn't imagine it could offer anything better. This would have been a perfect spot for a honeymoon.

But she had to stop thinking of that. Robert was dead. No matter what she thought she had seen back home, in the classroom and in the attic. He was gone, and she had to move forward. There was nothing to be gained by dwelling on the past. Except for hallucinating ghosts in the attic.

She took a deep breath. There were days when she still missed him so terribly that her body ached. She longed to touch him again, to have his naked body pressing against hers, to feel him moving inside her. Those were the times when she thought maybe she just needed a man, that maybe she should be like Amy and flirt with half the guys she came in contact with. But she didn't want just any man. She still wanted Robert.

"What'cha doing?" Amy stood in the doorway, pulling the tousled hair out of her eyes.

"Oh," she said, "just sitting here. Did I wake you?"

Amy rubbed her eyes with the heel of her hand. "No." She sank into the other rocker. "I got up to go to the bathroom and saw you were gone."

"It's nice out."

Amy closed her eyes and leaned her head back against the chair. "It's too fucking early." She yawned.

"David wasn't kidding about those nachos. I don't want any crab for a long time."

Sarah laughed. "Yeah, me, too."

Amy looked at her. "I've been thinking. We don't have to go today if you don't want to. I know you're kind of weirded out by the whole thing."

"I think I've just seen too many of those forensic science shows," Sarah said, and they giggled. "But if we get to the marina and find out he drives an old white van without any windows, I'm out of there."

Amy laughed. "Agreed."

As it turned out, the front desk clerk happily recommended Burke's Island Tours, which immediately set both their minds at ease. "I hear many good things about Mr. David," she told them. "You will have a good time."

And when they arrived at the marina a little before ten, several signs pointed the way to Slip 23. "Well, if he's going to murder us he might as well have a big flashing neon sign pointing to our bodies," Amy said.

When they reached the boat, David was on deck, leaning against the railing. He waved to them. "Ahoy, me mateys. Glad you decided to take me up on the offer." Sarah noticed he was considerably cleaner and neater than he had been at the pub, and now that she got a better look at him she could see why Amy thought he was attractive.

"We appreciate it," Amy said, leading the way up the ramp to the boat's deck.

It was a good-sized blue and white catamaran that gleamed from top to bottom, easy to see that David took great pride in it. "This is nice," Sarah said.

"Thanks." David pulled two bright orange life vests

from a storage bench and handed one to each of them. "One per customer."

"So how long does your typical tour last?" Amy asked, tying her vest.

"Around an hour and a half," David told her. "We go all the way around the island."

"You ladies better keep an eye on that wild man," said a voice from the big fishing boat next to them. Sarah looked up to see a dark-skinned man with corn rows and dark glasses watching them and smiling. "He's crazy."

David shook his head and smiled. "That's Eric," he told them. "He runs a fishing charter."

"I thought you were taking this week off," Eric said.

"I am," David said. "This is a personal excursion." He looked up toward Eric, shielding his eyes from the morning sun. "Why are you still here? Don't you have a charter today?"

"Canceled," Eric said. "Says he is sick or something."

"Must have had the crab nachos," Amy whispered, and Sarah giggled.

"That stinks," David said.

Eric shrugged and flashed a bright grin. "Not for me. No refunds."

"You want to come with us?" David asked him. He looked at Amy and Sarah. "You guys don't mind, do you?"

Sarah shook her head, and Amy said, "We don't mind."

"I'll even bring some refreshments," Eric said. "Special price for you, David. Five-ninety-nine each."

☠🎨☠

The day was rapidly growing warmer as they left the

harbor, and the sun beating down on the thick life vest made Sarah grateful for the cold bottle of Dasani David handed her. The sea was just as beautiful as ever, that bright vivid blue she couldn't get used to. Ben Harbour shrank as they moved toward the open water, a hodge-podge of pastel colors among the green foliage.

"You can see Main Street from here," David said from his spot behind the wheel. "As you've probably already noticed, golf carts are prevalent on the island. They're clean and quiet and keep the town from being congested, especially in the peak tourist season."

"When's peak season?" Amy asked above the thrum of the engine.

"Usually November through April."

"You get many people here on spring break?" Sarah asked.

"We do," David said. "But not many college kids. People that come here are usually families looking to avoid the drinking and partying that goes on in most of the other places."

"It seems kind of isolated here," Amy said. "I'm surprised there aren't any big resorts like at Nassau."

"Government decision," David said. "They want to keep the big hotel companies like Westin and Hilton out of here. They're afraid big resorts would ruin the atmosphere and character of the island."

"Makes sense," Amy said.

"Plus, like you said, it gives the place a feeling of isolation. Which means the small hotels and inns here can charge higher prices and keep things exclusive."

"Meaning they can cater to rich folks," Amy said.

David laughed. "You got it."

Ben Harbour now faded into the haze as the boat turned north. Though a few houses dotted the shore here, most of what they were seeing was the dense bushy growth of pine and palmettos stretching up into the dark hills.

"Not much to see on this end of the island," David said.

"This part has never been settled," Eric said.

"Why not?" Sarah asked.

"Too hilly and rocky for one thing. But according to legend, there are too many angry spirits there."

She thought of the zombie ritual video. "Are you talking about vodou?"

Eric pulled off his sunglasses and looked at her. "Yes. Of a sort."

David looked over his shoulder. "Vodou? Is that anything like voodoo? All that hocus-pocus and charms and stuff?"

"Voodoo is a sort of spin-off from vodou," Sarah said. "And they've both been misinterpreted over the years. I blame Hollywood."

"Isn't St. Celine a little too far east for that?" Amy said. "I thought the vodou religion was more prevalent around Haiti and south Florida."

"Ah," Eric said, "that is true. But you see before St. Celine was taken by the British and eventually became part of the Bahamas, it was founded by French refugees and their slaves from Haiti two hundred years ago. They were fleeing the slave revolt that eventually gained Haiti its independence."

"That explains all the French names," Amy said.

"They brought their culture with them," Eric said. "The slaves also brought their religion, a dark form of vodou which centers around the worship of Bacalou."

Sarah jumped. It was the name she had been trying to remember. The entity who had been depicted in the video. "He's one of the evil *loa*, isn't he?"

Eric looked at her, his eyes wide with surprise. "You know vodou?"

"I teach anthropology," she said. "I know about a lot of religions."

"Then you must know he is not one to play with. He is bad. Very bad."

"Are there still people on the island that practice this form of vodou?"

"Undoubtedly," Eric said. "But no one talks about it."

Sarah felt excitement in her chest. "Is there some way we could see a ceremony?" Eric's eyes narrowed, and she added quickly, "Strictly from an academic point of view. I don't want to interfere, I just want to observe."

Eric shook his head. "Absolutely not. Even if I knew someone who is involved in it – which I do *not* – there is no way I would be a party to it. It is very bad. Very dangerous."

Before she could stop herself, she blurted out, "What about zombies?" David turned to look at her, and Eric dropped his sunglasses. Amy gaped at her. Sarah swallowed. "I mean, is that part of the worship of Bacalou?"

Eric gave her a humorless grin. "You've seen the video on the internet, haven't you? The one supposedly made by the Canadian couple who disappeared."

"Yes," Sarah said. "I've seen it. Is it real?"

Eric blew out a breath. "Of course it's not real. No one knows where that video came from or how it got associated with St. Celine."

"But it was uploaded to Emily White's YouTube account the day before she went missing," Sarah said.

Eric shook his head. "Anyone with her password could have posted that. There is no proof she created the video or uploaded it. It was investigated thoroughly."

"The probe was still going on for months after I came down here," David said.

Amy leaned forward. "So what do you guys think happened to them?"

"I believe they left here and got into some trouble on their way home," Eric said, staring out at the island. "Just like the authorities said."

"I don't know," David said. "I got here in the middle of the investigation, so I can't really say. I just remember seeing some guys in suits in town that summer, and someone told me they were with the Canadian police."

"Yes," Eric said, "and they found nothing."

Sarah shook her head. "But from what I read, no one actually saw the Whites leave. No one at the inn, no one on the ferry."

"Don't forget," David said, "they never went through the airports either in Nassau or Eleuthera. The police looked through all the surveillance camera footage."

"There are other ways of leaving," Eric said. "Especially if you want to disappear."

"But they had no reason to do that," Sarah said. "They had friends and family. Jobs."

Eric shrugged. "What can I say? It is indeed a mystery."

David pointed off the bow of the boat. "Dolphins."

Sarah and Amy leaned out over the rail to get a better view. There were three of them, leaping out of the water and slicing through the air in big silver arcs, headed out to the open sea away from the island.

"I've never seen live dolphins before," Amy cried. She was snapping one picture after another with her phone as fast as her fingers would allow. "They're so beautiful!"

"Keep a sharp eye out," David said. "You might see a big stingray or two."

Sarah watched the water rush by the side of the boat. It was so clear she could see straight to the rocky bottom. A school of yellow fish darted away from their wake, appearing as a single shimmering mass among the brightly colored coral. "What are those?"

Eric leaned over and followed her gaze. "French grunts. They make a noise. Like grunting."

"Can you eat them?" Amy asked.

"You can," Eric said. "But they are small and full of bones. Too much trouble."

"So did you grow up here on St. Celine?" Sarah asked.

Eric slid his sunglasses back over his face. "Yes."

"Eric's descended from one of the original slave families that came here from Haiti," David said.

Sarah glanced back at Eric, who was studying the passing shoreline. "Really?"

"Most of us on the island are descended from slaves," he said, not looking at her. "Either the original ones from Haiti or later ones from Africa."

Sarah pulled the hair from her face and watched him. He didn't seem too interested in talking about St. Celine's past, but with slavery in his family history, who could blame him. She'd run into this a few times before, usually when talking about slavery in the United States to a classroom with a minority of African-American students. Some became defensive, especially toward her as a white woman. And while others joked casually about it, most seemed indifferent to it these days, seeing it as a period of history that didn't really affect them personally. Eric seemed almost ashamed, as if he had no desire to be associated with such a thing.

"What's that?" Amy said suddenly.

They had just rounded a small outcropping of rocks. A squat blue clapboard house with a rusted metal roof sat in a small clearing of pine and palm trees. Across the wide front porch stretched a white clothesline. Instead of clothes it was adorned with feathers and what appeared to be animal skins. Next to the house in the barren yard was a large pile of black stones. A small inverted red cross rose from it.

"We call that the witch's house," David said. "An old woman lives there. Mama Alice."

Sarah watched the house shrink from view and the realization suddenly dawned on her. "She's a vodou high priestess, isn't she?"

Eric took a deep breath and kept his gaze on the house. "So they say."

"Then you *do* know someone who practices vodou." Excitement blossomed in her chest. "I've got to meet her," she said. "I'd like to interview her."

"Oh, me, too," Amy said. She looked at Sarah. "That would make fabulous research."

Sarah looked at Eric. "Do you know her? Do you think you could introduce us?"

He turned to her, his eyes hidden by his dark glasses. "No. I could not do that."

"Oh, please," said Amy. "We just want to talk to her. See, I've been studying religions for several years and – "

"No!" He looked away as Amy shrank back. "I am . . . sorry, but it is out of the question. Leave Mama

Alice alone." His grip tightened on the chrome rail. "She is just an old woman and the victim of island rumors."

"I'm sorry," Sarah said. "We didn't mean to upset you."

"Stay away from there," Eric said, still watching the passing shoreline. "Promise me."

Sarah nodded. "All right." She caught David's eye. He shrugged. Amy shook her head, appearing baffled.

David cleared his throat. "And now, ladies and gentlemen," he said, launching into his tour guide voice, "if you will look to your right you will see the only natural waterfall in all the Bahamas, La Tour." Above them on the rocky slope was the cascading water, just as she had seen it in Josh and Emily's video.

"What river is that?" Amy asked.

"No river," said Eric. "It's a spring."

"Natural hot spring," David said. "It forms a pool at the base of the waterfall. Nice to sit in and relax."

"You've been there?" Amy asked.

He nodded. "Many times."

"Let's go there tomorrow," Sarah said to Amy. "I'd like to see it."

"Sounds fun," Amy said. She looked at David and Eric. "Would you two like to join us?"

"Thanks for the offer," Eric said, "but I have a full day scheduled." He smiled and nodded at David. "But I'm sure Todger would be happy to go."

David whirled and glared at him, his face growing red.

Sarah looked at the two men. "Todger?"

Eric burst out laughing.

"Shut up," David hissed at him, which made Eric laugh harder.

"Is that a nickname?" Sarah asked. Eric's infectious laughter coupled with the horrified expression on David's face was more than she could stand, and she started to giggle.

Amy was laughing, too. "I know what that means," she said.

David shot her a defeated glance. He pointed a finger at her. "Don't."

"Australian slang, isn't it?" she went on.

"Don't say it."

"It means, 'little penis,' doesn't it?" Amy said with a smirk.

Eric guffawed, and Sarah howled with laughter.

David hung his head and faced the front of the boat. His face was blood red.

Eric smacked Amy lightly on the shoulder. "You got it, girl!"

"The moral of this story is," David said above their laughter and staring straight ahead, "don't go to the men's room with an Australian bloke after you've been sitting on an ice chest for an hour."

7

As David helped her down the ramp, Amy smiled up at him. "Thanks for the tour. You've got to let us repay you somehow. For your hospitality." She had taken off her sunglasses, and her eyes were soft and brown.

"I couldn't," he said. "It was my pleasure."

"Come on," she said. She touched him on his bicep and he felt a thrill shoot through him. "Let us at least buy you dinner tonight."

He thought of what was waiting for him at home – the cat and probably a frozen entree – and found himself nodding. "Okay. I can do that."

"Is the food at the inn any good? We thought we might try the restaurant there tonight." She had a hint of a southern accent; funny he hadn't noticed it until now.

"I've been told it's the best on the island," he said. "Never been there myself."

She gave him a warm smile. "Now's your chance. Meet us in the lobby at six."

He nodded again. She was making it impossible to say no. "I'll be there."

As Amy and Sarah walked away, Eric ambled down the ramp behind him. "Bad business, my friend."

David glared at him. "Oh, shut up," he said.

Eric winked at him. "This from the man who said 'Never get involved with a tourist, it's a bad idea.'"

"I'm not involved," David said. He watched Amy and Sarah climb into their golf cart. They waved at him as they sped away and he lifted his hand in return. "No one's *involved*, it's just dinner."

Eric sauntered toward his boat, his hands in his pockets. "Uh huh."

"Hey, whatever, dude," David called after him. "Go back to your wife and kids. Let me stay home lonely and abandoned, I don't care."

Eric shot him the bird.

Later at home he fussed over what to wear. He hadn't been anywhere nice in a long time, and he wondered whether his good khakis would still fasten around his growing belly. They did – just barely. He decided to forgo the belt and leave his shirt untucked. That would at least hide the fat spilling over the waistband. He ran a wet hand through his hair and smoothed down his beard, brushed his teeth and applied deodorant. This wasn't a date, but he still wanted to be presentable. He was just turning from the mirror when a long stray eyebrow hair caught his eye. He grabbed it between his thumb and forefinger and plucked it out with a quick jerk, bringing tears to his eyes. Damn, beauty was painful.

He was a bit early to the inn, but was surprised to see Amy and Sarah already waiting for him. He was also surprised at how much he was actually looking forward to this, a night out. A rare thing for him these days.

Amy was wearing a white strapless dress which showed off her tanned shoulders and toned legs. Sarah was equally dazzling in a light blue mini-dress that perfectly complemented her lighter skin and blond hair. "You guys look great," he said.

"You clean up rather well yourself, Mr. Burke," Sarah said.

Amy laughed. "Are we just going to gawk at one another or are we going to eat? I'm starving."

When they were seated and served with a bottle of white wine, David surveyed the menu and felt a sting of shock. There was nothing less than forty dollars. "Wow, I can't let you pay for mine."

Amy took a small sip from her glass. "Don't be ridiculous. I saw what you charge for a tour. We're getting off cheap."

David laughed. "I guess you are at that."

"So," Sarah said, "you never told us what you did before you came to the island."

"Let me guess," Amy said. "Professional fisherman."

David laughed. "No. Try again."

"Hhmm," Sarah said, studying his face. "You said you were from Indiana, so I'm going to guess farmer. Corn maybe."

David shook his head. "You're both wrong. I'm an ex-banker." He laughed at their surprised expressions. "Hard to believe, isn't it?"

"So what'd you do," Amy said, "make your millions and retire to the Bahamas?"

"Something like that," he said. He told them about the stress, the panic attacks, the feeling that life was flying past him while he sat hunkered down day after day with pages of numbers. "It was time to get out. Time to live a little."

Sarah nodded. "I admire that. Going after your dream, that takes. . ."

"Balls," Amy finished for her, and they all laughed.

Sarah raised her wineglass. "Here's to balls."

They all clinked their glasses together. "To balls!"

☠︎☠︎☠︎

After dinner, they headed down the trail to the beach. The sun was just hitting the horizon and the light was warm and golden. A fresh breeze blew in from the water and a few gulls shrieked overhead. Amy and Sarah took off their shoes and begged him to do the same. He had to admit, the hot dry sand felt good between his toes. He didn't get to the beach often, and when he did he always wondered what had kept him away.

"I meant what I said today," Amy told him, "about hiking up to La Tour tomorrow. We'd like you to come with us."

"Oh, no," he said, "I don't want to butt in on your trip."

Amy laughed and shook her head. "You're not butting in. We'd like you to come. Wouldn't we, Sarah?"

"Of course," Sarah said, but something in her tone told David she wasn't being completely honest.

"I've got so much at home I need to do," he said. "I don't get the chance to do much work on the house during tourist season."

"But you said you're taking this week off," Amy said. "Come on with us tomorrow. You'll still have the rest of the week for chores."

"Well. . ." He looked at Sarah. "Are you sure you don't mind, Sarah?"

"I don't mind," she said. "It's nice having our own tour guide." She gave a smile that seemed genuine, and he guessed he must have imagined the hesitancy in her voice before.

He blew out a breath. "Okay, I'll go."

Amy grinned. "Great. It'll be fun."

"Wear sturdy shoes," he told them. "The path is kind of rocky. And bring your swimsuits. You'll want to get in that water once you get there."

Amy saluted him. "Aye aye, captain."

8

Sarah lay sleepless in her bed. The ceiling fan was going full tilt, but she was suffocating. She threw off the covers and lay there under the breeze, feeling the sweat on her skin turn cold and clammy in the darkness.

She was pissed at Amy. This was supposed to be their trip. Just the girls. Just the two of them exploring the island and having adventures together. Now she had brought David into the mix.

It wasn't that she didn't like David. He was friendly and easygoing, and fun to talk with. But she could see Amy's growing attraction for him at dinner – why she couldn't guess – and Sarah had begun to feel awkward. And she could tell David sensed it, too. But David was eating it up, just like any man would.

She supposed, knowing what Amy had told her about her past, that it wasn't unexpected. Just disappointing. They had come here to forget about life. And

Sarah was hoping to finally erase Robert's memory or whatever had caused her hallucinations back home. But it was going to be harder now that she would have to watch Amy falling for some guy they had just met.

A cry from outside filled the room, sounding like an injured cat, loud and shrill in the blackness beyond the open verandah doors.

Amy sat straight up in the next bed, clutching the sheets to her chest. "What the fuck was that?"

The cry came again, louder this time, answered by another in the distance.

Sarah sat up. "Relax, it's just the peacocks."

"Are you sure?" Amy said. "It sounds like a baby crying."

"I'm sure," Sarah said. "You've never heard peacocks before?"

"No. That's creepy as *fuck*." The distant peacock called again and Amy flopped back down on the bed. "How's anybody supposed to sleep with that going on?"

Sarah climbed out of bed. "Here, I'll close the doors."

"Please do."

She stepped cautiously through the dark room, barking her shin on an ottoman in the process, until she reached the open doors. The breeze flowing in was cool and dry, and she hated to close it off. She stepped out onto the balcony and looked below for the peacocks in the moonlight, but there was no sign of them. They had evidently bedded down for the night, and she wondered if something had startled them.

She had just turned to go back inside when movement on the walkway below caught her attention. A man was standing next to one of the thick palm trees.

She could see the silhouette in the half-light given off by the lamppost close to the inn's back deck. Was it one of the workers from the inn? Another guest? Or was it one of her hallucinations? The form wasn't moving. It stood like a stone. She couldn't tell which direction he was facing. Was he watching her? Could he see her up on the verandah staring at him?

She turned her head toward the room, keeping her eyes fixed on the figure. "Amy," she whispered. "Amy!"

Amy groaned. "What?"

"Come out here. There's somebody out here. In the garden."

"What?"

"It's a man. I think he's watching me."

"Are you crazy?" But Amy appeared beside her in seconds. "Where?"

Sarah pointed. "See him?"

Amy gave a slight gasp. "Yes," she whispered.

"What's he doing?"

Amy moved closer to Sarah. "He's just standing there."

"I wonder if he stirred up the peacocks," Sarah said.

The figure's arm moved, and they both spotted the glow of a cigarette. It brightened as the man inhaled, then disappeared from view again below the foliage.

"Let's go back in," Amy whispered. "This is freaking me out."

Inside, Sarah double checked to make sure the doors were locked, then crawled back into bed, pulling the covers up to her chin. She was suddenly chilled. A thought struck her. "Amy, you don't think that was David, do you?"

"What would David be doing here in the middle of

the night?"

"I don't know," Sarah said. "What if he's some kind of stalker?"

Amy blew out a breath. "It's probably some clerk from the front desk out for a smoke break."

Sarah lay silent and still until she heard Amy begin to snore softly. Amy was right of course. She was psyching herself into a panic. It could have been anyone from the inn. Maybe even a maintenance worker.

But one thing did ease her mind: Amy had seen him, too.

9

When she saw David waiting in the lobby the next morning, Amy's first thought was, *Oh my God, he* does *look like Larry the Cable Guy*. He was wearing a faded red ball cap and a sleeveless t-shirt with the Indiana University logo on it. He also had on blue swimming trunks and a pair of well-worn hiking boots. She noticed he had a tribal tattoo around his left bicep. The edges were black and sharp, and she wondered if it was fairly new, something he had done once he left his old life behind. He looked up from his newspaper and gave them a wide grin. "Hey."

Amy looked down at her tennis shoes. "Will these be okay? Neither of us have any boots."

"You'll be fine," he said. "As long as you're not wearing sandals or flip-flops." He looked them up and down. "Swimsuits?"

Sarah twisted into a model pose. "Underneath our clothes."

Outside the morning sun was hot. David pulled a bottle from his backpack. "Water?"

Amy nodded toward the shoulder bags she and Sarah were carrying. "We've got some. Thanks."

At the edge of the garden a worn path wound up the hill and disappeared around a bend into the scrub forest. A sign pointed the direction toward La Tour, a mile and a half away.

"Pretty good trek," David said.

"Let's go," Sarah said.

David grinned at them and led the way. "I don't want to hear any complaints," he said. "You'll get tired, but the reward is worth it. I promise."

They moved farther into the growth of ferns and palmettos. The path led through a stand of tall palms, but they provided relatively little shade from the sun. Amy took a sip of water. She could already feel sweat trickling down her neck. Behind her, Sarah's face was red and her hair was wet and frizzy. "You okay, Sarah?"

"Fine." She pressed her water bottle against her forehead. "Wouldn't think it would be this hot so early in the day."

"Welcome to the tropics, my dear," David said.

Amy watched his ass as he climbed the trail. It was nice and plump beneath his swim trunks, and she wondered how it would feel to grab onto. His legs were covered in fine reddish-brown hair and his calves were well-muscled and defined. She watched his legs move, watched the muscles relax and contract. Yep. Nothing like Tim's scrawny-ass chicken legs. David's arms were solid, but not too beefy, ending in hands that were rough and calloused, with fingers that were thick and topped with large square nails. She tried to imagine those hands shuffling papers in a bank and couldn't do it. Those hands were meant to be outside. They were supposed to be doing physical labor, not penciling figures into columns. She wondered how they would feel on her skin and a tingle of pleasure rippled through her. The name Eric had called him – "Todger" – floated through her head and she held back a giggle, wondering if it was true. She decided it didn't matter; Tim had been fairly well-endowed but still hadn't known what to do with it. Besides, she didn't figure she would get the chance to find out.

"How you guys doing back there?" David asked, looking over his shoulder.

"Great," Amy said.

"Sarah?"

"I'm okay," Sarah said behind her.

"Let me know if I need to slow down or if you need to take a breather," he said. "We're about halfway there."

"I'm good," Sarah said.

"There's an overlook just around this next bend," he told them. "Great view of the beach and the town."

He was right. A rocky outcropping jutted out over the dense forest and just below that, pink sand stretched beside the turquoise water. In the distance, they could make out Ben Harbour through the haze and the open sea beyond. A white shape appeared on the water, moving closer to town. "There's the ferry," David said.

Beside her, Sarah snapped a picture with her phone. "You must love it here," she said. "Robert would have really liked this place."

Amy felt a spark of irritation, and David said, "Who's Robert?"

"He was my fiancé," Sarah said, staring out at the

view. "He died last November."

"Oh," David said. "Sorry to hear about that."

"It's one of the reasons we wanted to come on this trip," Amy told him. "Sarah needed to get away. We'd both worked hard all semester. We needed a reward."

David took a swig from his water bottle. "So. . . any fiancés in your life?"

"No," Amy said. "Just one stupid rat-bastard of an ex-husband."

David's eyes widened. "All righty then."

"It's been a couple years," she said, hoping she hadn't come off as an angry psycho divorcee. "We don't communicate. He's in Texas."

"Ah." He adjusted his cap and wiped his forehead with the back of his hand. She thought she detected just a hint of a smile, but then he turned away, back toward the path. "Ready when you guys are."

"Let's go," Sarah said, following behind David.

Amy took one last look at the view and grabbed a picture with her phone, then headed back to the path.

They hadn't gone far when an older couple, a tall man in jean shorts and an orange t-shirt and a woman in aqua capris and a bikini top, appeared around the turn. They were giggling and hanging on to each other like teenagers, though they had to be close to sixty. "Hi!" the woman said. "Going up?"

"Yes we are," David said.

"How is it?" Sarah asked.

"It's beautiful up there!" the woman gushed.

The man ran his fingers through his graying hair. "We're on our honeymoon," he said, grinning and winking at David.

Amy saw the smile fade from Sarah's face, and she quickly said, "Congratulations."

"Thanks!" the woman said as they passed by. "You kids have fun!"

Amy watched them disappear down the path. "Thank you."

Sarah shifted the bag on her shoulder. "Let's get a move-on, Captain," she said.

David looked at her, then caught Amy's eye. "Sure."

10

They heard the water long before they saw it. A steady, pulsing roar. And once the path emerged from the forest and the waterfall came into view, Sarah's breath left her. The ribbon of water cascaded from the rocky cliff above, thundering into the pool below. She could feel the power of it in her chest, through her whole body. It was vibrant and intoxicating.

"Come on!" Amy cried, wriggling out of her t-shirt and shorts.

David unshouldered his backpack and began untying his boots. He looked at Sarah. "You okay?" he said above the din of the water.

She managed a smile. "I'm good."

He stepped out of the boots and tossed his cap to the ground. "You getting in?"

She nodded. "Of course." She set down her bag and slipped out of her sneakers.

Behind them, Amy was already wading into the pool. "It's cold! Why is it so cold? I thought it was a hot spring."

"It cools down once it comes over the falls," David said. He peeled off his shirt and headed toward the water. His back was hairy, and Sarah felt a twinge of revulsion.

She turned away from them and pulled out of her t-shirt and slid her shorts down her legs. The ground was hot and dry to her bare feet, but she could feel the cool mist from the waterfall on her bare shoulders. She folded her clothes and placed them on top of the bag, then took a quick sip of water. In the pool, David and Amy were splashing each other. Amy was squealing.

Josh and Emily's video replayed in her head. *Get in the water, it's great!* And then the comment on the blog: *For God's sake, Em.*

"Come on!" Amy called to her. "It feels wonderful!"

Sarah stepped into the pool. The water was cool, but not as cold as she was expecting. But after the hot climb up the path it was invigorating. The water was crystal clear. She could see her toes on the rocky bottom. Soon she was laughing and splashing with Amy and David. She wished she could be as unselfconscious about her body as David seemed to be. He was kind of fat, for crying out loud, and he wasn't trying to hide anything. She supposed it was the same modesty that had persuaded her to buy the one-piece suit that now kept her in the water up to her chin. She finally found a ledge at the end of the pool and reclined on it, watching Amy and David continue to cavort in the cascade. Honestly, if Amy wasn't careful her boobs were going to pop right out of that bikini top. And maybe that's what she wanted, to give David an eyeful.

She knew she was being a petty bitch. It wasn't David's fault. It wasn't anyone's fault, not even Amy's. Amy was just having a good time. A good time like Sarah was supposed to be having. Why couldn't she just let go and enjoy herself? It was like high school all over again, the popular girls flirting with all the guys and the guys fawning all over them. She had never considered herself pretty, though she had never failed to attract her share of attention. Robert had even called her beautiful. But Robert had been in love with her. She realized she was jealous of Amy, that only Amy could come to an island fifteen hundred miles away and attract the only eligible man around. And what had David seen in Amy that he hadn't seen in Sarah?

Amy wasn't moping around after a dead fiancé for one thing. She was spirited and fun-loving. Outgoing and friendly. And try as she might, Sarah would never be able to reach that level of vivacity. It just wasn't in her.

After an eternity, David and Amy dragged themselves out of the water, and Sarah followed. The sun seemed hotter than ever, and her arms tingled. She toweled off and sprayed on more sunscreen. She hoped she wouldn't burn.

David pulled on his shirt and dug through his backpack. "Anybody hungry? I've got some granola bars."

"I'll take one," Sarah said, stepping into her shorts. She hadn't realized how hungry she was until David mentioned food, and now her stomach rumbled. He tossed one to her. It was peanuts and honey, not her favorite, but it would do.

Amy had already tied her shoes and was wandering around the clearing. She pointed toward a path that entered the forest opposite the way they had come. "David, do you know where this leads to?"

He shook his head. "No clue. This is the farthest I've ever been."

Amy was tying her hair back into a ponytail. "Anyone up for an adventure?"

Sarah swallowed the bite of granola bar and said, "I am," surprising herself.

David shrugged. "Sure."

The path led down a rocky slope covered with scrub forest, much denser than on the other side of the waterfall. Here the trail was hard to make out and wasn't nearly as worn.

"Careful," David said as he inched along ahead of them. "There's some loose rock here. I'd hate for one of you to turn an ankle. Not sure I could carry you all the way back to the inn."

At that moment, Sarah's feet flew out from beneath her and she landed hard on her behind. Her breath left her and her wrist screamed with pain where she had scraped it on a rock.

Amy was on her at once. "Oh my God, Sarah, are you all right?"

David extended his hand and helped her back to her feet. "I'm okay," she said, her face burning with embarrassment.

"Maybe we should go back," David said.

"I'm all right," Sarah told him. She was getting tired of them acting like she was made of glass. "Let's keep going."

"Where do you think this leads to?" Amy asked.

David looked around. "We're on the north end of the island. It probably leads down to the water. One of those rocky points I showed you from the boat yesterday."

"I'd like to see that," Sarah said.

Amy nodded. "Yeah, me, too."

David turned around and headed back down the trail. "Let's go, then."

A little farther along the forest suddenly cleared and the vivid blue water came into view. The beach was lined with massive boulders rounded over time by wind and waves, and Sarah was reminded of the giant statues lining the shores of Easter Island in the Pacific. The breeze here was hot and strong, stirring the towering palms in the forested hills behind them. Farther out, the water turned a darker blue beneath a cobalt sky dotted with massive white clouds. The surf was stronger here than on the beach at the inn, and Sarah realized it was because there was no natural breakwater to soften the waves.

"Wow," David said. "I've never been here before, although I've seen it from the boat. It looks different up close."

Amy thrust her phone at Sarah. "Take my picture," she said. She climbed atop one of the larger rocks and posed.

"Pretend you're a mermaid," Sarah said.

Amy pursed her lips duck-style and rolled her eyes toward the clouds.

"Hey," David said. "I know where we are. We're not far from the witch house."

Amy sat up atop the rock. "Oh, let's go there," she said.

"I don't know," Sarah said.

"Yeah," David said, "Eric made you promise you'd stay away from Mama Alice's place and not bother her."

"We won't bother her," Amy said. "We just want to talk to her."

"Let's not," Sarah said.

"Oh come on, Sarah. Yesterday you were all for it." She jumped down to the sand. "Which way is it?"

David took a deep breath and pointed. "That way."

Amy headed off down the beach. "Come on."

David shot Sarah a *can-you-believe-this* look and followed Amy. Sarah watched them for a moment, then trailed behind them. "Wait up," she said.

Around the next outcropping was the clearing and Mama Alice's house. White chickens pecked at the ground next to the forest, and Sarah could hear them clucking. The skins and feathers hanging on the porch looked dirty and matted now that she could see them closer, and the blue paint on the wooden clapboards was faded and peeling. The front door stood wide open, covered by a screen, and she thought she saw movement in the darkness behind it.

"I don't like this," Sarah said. "Let's go back."

"I'm with Sarah," David said. "I feel like we're trespassing."

Amy rolled her eyes at them. "Relax, you two." She marched up toward the front steps. "Hello?"

On the other side of the house was a chopping block covered with dried blood and feathers. An ax was embedded in it, blade down. Next to it was the pile of black rocks topped with the inverted red cross she had seen from the boat. She moved closer. The cross wasn't exactly red. It was more of a rusty brown color. Painted on in several layers. She reached out to it. It didn't exactly look like paint. It looked more like blood.

"Can I help you children?"

Sarah whirled around. A large dark-skinned woman in a faded red sundress and a kerchief had come around from behind the house. She looked at them without expression.

Amy stepped off the porch. "Are you Mama Alice?"

The woman gave a single nod. "I am."

"My name's Amy Vandiver." She extended her hand. Mama Alice looked at it, but made no effort to take it. Amy lowered her hand. "These are my friends, Sarah Dunham and David Burke. We saw your house from the water yesterday and wanted to meet you." She glanced quickly at David, then back at Mama Alice. "Eric sent us."

Mama Alice blinked. "Eric? Eric Durand?"

"That's right," David said. "I operate a tour boat. You've probably seen me go by – "

"I know who you are," Mama Alice said. "St. Celine is small. I know everyone." She took a seat on the edge of the porch. "I don't get much company way out here. Forgive me if I'm not very hospitable."

"We don't mean to intrude," Sarah said. "We just wanted to talk with you a bit. We. . ."

"We wanted to ask you about vodou," Amy blurted.

Mama Alice looked at her and sighed. "I figured as much. You want me to stir up a charm for you, right? What is it? Love? Money? Revenge?"

"No," Amy said. "It's nothing like that." She sat down beside Mama Alice. "Sarah and I are college instructors – sociology and anthropology. We're interested in the religion from an academic standpoint. I've been studying religions for years. I've interviewed people of every kind of faith imaginable. I – " she glanced at Sarah – "that is, *we* would like to see a ceremony."

"We don't want to intrude," Sarah said. "We'd just like to observe."

Mama Alice looked at the ground. "I see."

"We promise not to get in the way," Amy said. "We just want to take notes, maybe take a few photos – "

"No!" Mama Alice's face had become hard. "There would absolutely be no photographs."

Amy locked glances with Sarah, then looked back at Mama Alice. "Sure. No photos."

"Let me explain something," Mama Alice said. "*If* I give you permission to see a ceremony, you will have to abide by certain rules."

"Of course," Sarah said.

"Vodou is very misunderstood." She looked at them. "There are very few people on the island who practice it, and they do not want outsiders watching them, expecting what they have seen in movies and on TV."

"We understand," Amy said. "We'll stay out of the way."

"You will hide yourselves in the brush," Mama Alice said. "No one must see you. If the congregation dis-covers you, things could get. . . ugly."

Sarah thought of Emily's video, of the way it ended abruptly. A cold sweat broke out on her forehead. Is that what had happened to them? Had someone seen them and attacked them? Maybe followed them back to the inn? And if so, did she want to take the same risk?

"I can't allow you to take any photographs that might end up God-knows-where for all the world to see." She leaned in close to Sarah, and her eyes were black and narrow. "*You* do not want that to happen, either."

"So," Amy said, "if we agree to your terms, stay out

of sight and no photographs, can we watch a ceremony."

Mama Alice took a deep breath. "You may. But I must warn you, if you are seen I will not be responsible for what happens to you. I will deny inviting you."

Amy looked at Sarah, then back at Mama Alice. "Okay. We understand."

"There will be a ceremony tonight. I will tell you how to get there. You must never tell anyone else where the temple is located."

"We won't," Amy said.

"The ceremony will start at nine and last until morning. You must come after dark and leave before the ceremony ends so no one will see you."

"We can do that," Sarah said. She was excited now. "We promise we'll do everything you ask."

II

Mama Alice watched the three strangers disappear behind the rocks, back the way they had come. So Eric Durand had sent them, had he? She must remember to caution him about outsiders. That was how the Bad Business happened two summers ago.

She stood and stretched her back. It was aching. There would be rain in the next few days.

She grabbed a small crate made of wood and wire and shuffled around the house toward the chickens. She would need two for tonight, a cock and a hen. And a third for her dinner this evening. The water was already boiling in the pot out back.

None of her three visitors were sinless. The dark-haired one was especially vile, and Mama Alice could tell she had already charmed Mr. David. From what Eric had told her, he was a good man and smart, but since he was a man he was not immune to the wicked ways of a vixen. Now the fair one was different. She'd had only one lover in her life and so retained a portion of her purity. And she was a rare breed, light-haired and pale-skinned. She hadn't noticed when Mama Alice had picked a stray blond hair from her shoulder and slid it into the wide pocket of her house dress, a blond hair that would be used tonight when the *loa* would be summoned.

The fair one would make an excellent offering to Bacalou.

12

That was weird," David said as they headed back up the rocky path toward La Tour. "I can't believe you two are actually considering this."

Amy followed him, this time trying not to stare at his ass. "But it's a once-in-a-lifetime chance," she said. "I've always wanted to see an authentic vodou ceremony."

"I really wish you hadn't brought Eric's name into it."

"Sorry about that. I panicked. It was all I could think to say."

"Amy," Sarah said behind her, "do you think this is how Josh and Emily got in trouble?"

Amy blew out a breath. She was really starting to tire of this Josh and Emily shit. "I don't know," she said. "So they might have gone to see a ceremony. Maybe they got too close and got caught. That doesn't mean that's why they disappeared. Hell, you might as well say they vanished because they went to La Tour, or because they took a boat ride. Nobody knows, Sarah."

"You don't have to be nasty about it," Sarah said.

"I'm not trying to be nasty," Amy told her.

"Sarah does have a point," David said. "I was more than a little creeped out by that whole conversation with Mama Alice." He looked over his shoulder. "And that whole business about 'I won't be responsible for what happens to you.' I didn't like that at all."

Amy shook her head. "Fine. If you two don't want to go, I'll just go by myself."

"No!" David and Sarah both said at the same time.

"If you go, *I'll* go," Sarah said.

David stopped walking and turned around. "You two aren't going by yourselves. I'll go with you."

Amy smiled at him. It was cute how protective he was of them suddenly.

He noticed her stare and smiled back. "I mean, if someone *should* happen to see you, it would be better if you're with a local. So they'll know you're not just some strangers lurking around. I may know some of the people there and I can talk to them."

"That does make sense," Amy said.

"And I don't relish the idea of the two of us blundering around by ourselves in the dark," Sarah added.

"Ah," David said, "so there'll be *three* of us blundering around by ourselves in the dark."

By the time they reached La Tour, Amy felt as if her thighs would explode. The heat and constant stress of climbing the path of loose rock seemed to have taken a toll on all of them, and they collapsed at the edge of the pool. "What say we take a quick dip in the water before we head back down?" she said.

David had already pulled off his boots and socks. "Thought you'd never ask," he said.

They sat quietly in the pool this time, not splashing or chasing each other, just listening to the roar of the waterfall and feeling the spray on their faces. Above them, the sky had turned a deeper blue, and the clouds drifted lazily toward the east.

"What time is it?" Sarah asked.

"I looked at my phone when we got back here and it was almost two," Amy told her.

"I'm starved," Sarah said.

"Me, too," David said. "I've still got some granola bars left."

"I want some real food," Amy said, "like a thick steak and a baked potato."

"That sounds wonderful," Sarah said. "With something gooey and chocolate for dessert."

"I've got an idea," David said. "How about letting me cook for you guys tonight? I'm pretty handy with a grill."

Amy glanced at Sarah, then looked at David. "Really? You sure you want to do that?"

"I'd love to," he said. "You can come to my place, we'll have dinner, and then we'll head out and find this vodou temple."

"Sounds fun," Amy said. She loved a man who could cook. Especially when he had a great ass.

13

David heard the golf cart putter up the drive, and he made a last quick nervous glance at himself in the bathroom mirror before meeting Amy and Sarah at the front door. "Right on time," he said to them.

Amy pulled her hair back. Her face was flushed and expectant. "Your road is shit," she said. "I thought I'd accidentally turned down an old creek bed."

He held the door open for them. "Yeah, I should have warned you about that." They stepped into the living room, and David caught a hint of Amy's scent, a mixture of warm vanilla and coconut.

"Cute place," Sarah said.

"Thanks," David said. "It's small, but it's comfortable."

"Sarah's got an old Victorian," Amy said. "I keep telling her it's bigger than my whole apartment complex."

"Robert and I were working on restoring it," Sarah said. She looked away.

"Steaks are on the grill," David said, sensing her discomfort. "You two want something to drink? Wine? Heineken? Soda?"

"I'll take a beer," Amy said.

Sarah shook her head. "I'm good right now." She sat down awkwardly on the edge of the sofa, as if she were afraid of getting too comfortable.

Amy took the beer from David and sipped it. "Nice vinyl collection you got there."

David grunted as he piled salad onto three plates. "Thanks. It was real chore getting it all here."

Amy perused the shelves. "I've got a small collection," she said. "Nothing like this."

"What kind of stuff do you like?" David asked.

"'Fifties jazz, Sinatra, Julie London, that kind of thing." She pulled out an album. "Hey, Brubeck." She looked at him. "Can we?"

"Sure," he said. He put the record on the turntable and piano, sax, bass and drums were soon involved in a lively conversation. "I don't meet too many people who know what a vinyl record looks like, let alone who Dave Brubeck is."

"My grandmother left me her records," Amy said. "I used to play them all the time when I stayed at her house. I don't listen to them much anymore, but when I do it brings back good memories." She nodded to the beat of the music. "This was always one of my favorites."

"What about you, Sarah?" David asked. "Why kind of music do you like?"

"Oh, everything," she said. "No vinyl in my house, I'm afraid, but Robert had a ton of big band CDs. He really liked Glenn Miller. And Benny Goodman." She looked up at him. "I think I'll take some wine after all."

☠ ☠ ☠

Outside, the early evening air was cool and dry, and they sat about the table on the deck enjoying their meal. Seymour made an appearance, though he usually hid from strangers, and let Amy and Sarah scratch him behind the ears before he darted off into the brush. The steaks were perfect, the wine crisp and cold, and after dinner the conversation flowed like the three of them were old friends.

"So tell us about your brother," Amy said. "Is he anything like you?"

David began gathering their empty plates. "No, we're nothing alike." He led the way back into the kitchen and set the dishes in the sink. "He's still the golden child of finance." He flipped on the coffee maker. "And the apple of my parents' eyes."

Sarah slid into a seat at the dining table. "I sense a bit of hostility," she said with a smile.

David chuckled and pulled a chocolate pie from the refrigerator, the one he'd bought at the A&A Market. "I really try to hide that," he said.

"Has he been down to visit you?" Amy asked.

"Um, no. That would require some effort on his part, and time taken away from his precious job."

"I see." Amy took a seat opposite Sarah. "What about your parents?"

"I've tried several times to get them to come down, but they don't travel much. Plus my dad seems to think I'm wasting my life here, so something tells me it wouldn't be a very friendly visit."

"So who's the girl?" Amy was pointing to a photo

held onto the refrigerator with a magnet. It was a picture of him and Beth standing in front of a Mickey Mouse topiary at Disney World. He had put it up right after moving in and had promptly forgotten about it; no longer even saw it, in fact.

"My ex-fiancée," he said. "She didn't want to make the move from Indy. I didn't want to stay there. We reached an impasse. I had to decide between her and coming down here."

Amy leaned back in her chair. "Sounds like you made the right decision."

14

At ten the three of them left David's house on foot and headed up the rutted gravel road following the directions Mama Alice had given them. Sarah was glad to be doing something finally; watching Amy and David flirt was getting on her nerves. She was already anxious in anticipation of the ceremony and the caffeine in the coffee hadn't helped matters. And Amy and David's inane conversation about their families and past loves had droned on forever. A dull throb had begun behind Sarah's eyes; she would be lucky if she didn't end up with a migraine.

David led the way, illuminating the road with a flashlight. The pines and palms on either side of them rose up into blackness like the walls of a cave, and the constant whir of insects was nearly deafening. After all the walking earlier in the day, Sarah's legs were nearly like rubber, and just when she felt she couldn't go any farther, the light caught a narrow dirt lane that intersected the gravel road.

"This must be it," David said. He shined the light ahead of them. The lane was two ruts in the sandy soil with a strip of brown grass between them.

"I hear something," Amy said.

And then Sarah heard it, too. Drums. Pounding an incessant, driving rhythm. The sound came from somewhere ahead of them in the blackness. "Let's go," she said.

Farther up the lane and around a bend, the forest cleared a bit, and an orange glow could be seen through the trees. David doused the flashlight. The illumination from up ahead was enough to watch their footing. "This way," he whispered, weaving them through a stand of palmettos toward the brilliance and the pounding drums ahead.

At the edge of the brush, the three of them knelt and peered through the foliage at the scene in front of them. "Wow," Amy said, her voice barely audible above the driving beat.

The temple was an open-air pavilion strung with a web of bare bulbs. A large bonfire blazed to one side with a flickering glow. Several dark-skinned men beat relentlessly on large drums at one end of the temple, accompanied by two women with rattles and bells, and a group of worshippers sang and chanted in unison as they swayed and danced in a circle around a tall wooden pole. Along a far wall several tables were set up, aglow with candles and adorned with colorful swaths of fabric; they bowed with the weight of liquor bottles and pots and casserole dishes.

Sarah felt her breath catch in her throat; this was the place in the video. She and Amy exchanged glances, and she knew Amy recognized it as well.

For several minutes the proceedings continued unabated. A thin man wearing a straw hat bent down at the base of the pole and began drawing symbols using a white powder. Whether it was salt or flour, Sarah couldn't tell. The drums intensified, their rhythm growing faster. She could feel them in her chest, in her head, under her feet.

Suddenly a young man in khakis and a white shirt danced away from the crowd, toward the center pole. His arms and legs shook violently and his eyes were wide and wild. He whirled and danced, crashing into other participants, who grabbed him by the shoulders and thrust him back into the open. At no time did the singing and chanting stop.

David leaned in close to Sarah. "Do you have any idea what the hell is going on?"

Sarah laughed. "The drums and songs are to invoke the spirits – the *loa* – to make their presence known. One by one the *loa* will come into the circle and mount a member of the congregation."

He frowned. "Mount?"

"Sort of like possession. That guy spinning around has just been mounted."

They watched as two other men guided him back toward the tables. One of them poured a shot from a bottle and put it to the younger man's lips. He drank it in a single gulp, then moved back toward the center of the circle.

"They offer gifts to the *loa*," Sarah whispered to David, "like food and alcohol."

"Keep watching," Amy said. "They'll probably sacrifice an animal."

"Animal?" David said with alarm.

Sarah nodded. "Usually a chicken or a goat."

After a few more minutes, a woman appeared with a

crate bearing two chickens – a white hen and a black rooster. It was Mama Alice. She pulled out the hen and gave it to the man in the straw hat. He took the hen by the feet and swung it in an arc. The hen's wings flapped slightly. The drums continued to pound. A woman poured out a few grains of corn in the center of the drawn symbols, and the man in the hat set the hen down before them. The hen pecked at the corn. The man raised the hen above his head and the bird spread its wings. The singing grew louder and the dancing quickened. Suddenly, he grabbed the chicken by the head and whirled it, wringing its neck. He dropped it, and the hen flopped on the ground with lifeless spasms.

Sarah looked back at Mama Alice. She gasped.

Mama Alice was looking right at them, as if she could see them hiding in the brush. Sarah's blood felt ice cold in her veins. Mama Alice smiled.

"I think we better leave," Sarah said. "Mama Alice sees us."

"I think you're right," David said. "Come on."

They backed slowly away from their hiding place, turning back toward the dirt lane. Now ahead of them was utter darkness. David switched on the flashlight, covering most of the beam so that only a tiny pin-prick of light came through his fingers. "Follow me," he said. "Hold on to each other."

They inched away from the activity and the incessant drums, into the black void of the forest ahead. Suddenly Sarah bumped into Amy in front of her. She realized David had stopped. The light shone on the ground ahead, illuminating something blocking the path.

It was bare feet.

David swung the light upward and shone it on the round black face. It was a girl, no more than twelve, standing like a stone facing them. Her eyes were milky white.

Before she could stop herself, Sarah screamed.

"Come on," David cried, pulling them past the girl and on toward the dirt lane.

Leaves and brambles tore at Sarah's arms and legs as she ran blindly behind David and Amy. In a moment, they reached the dirt road and stopped there, gasping for breath. David shined the light at the edge of the forest. There was nothing but palm leaves and dense brush.

"Did she follow us?" Amy said

David was bent over, a hand on one knee as he struggled to catch his breath. "I don't think so."

"Did you see her *eyes*?" Amy said. "What was wrong with her fucking eyes?"

"I think she was blind," David said. He stood up-right and took a few deep breaths. "Let's get back to the house."

But Sarah stood rooted to the spot. A cold realization had come over her. "Do you know who that was?" she said. "It was the little girl from the zombie video."

15

Back at David's, the three of them sat at the kitchen table, doctoring their wounds. Amy swabbed a particularly nasty cut across her shin; the alcohol-drenched cotton ball was like fire. *"Shit!"*

David motioned to his open Heineken. "The beer helps," he said. He was sporting a gash across his cheek that Amy had cleaned and smeared with antibiotic ointment. He had been so cute, wincing as she dabbed the cut with the cotton ball. She caught his gaze at one point, and she wondered if he was somehow enjoying it. She jabbed the cotton ball into his cheek and he let out a yell. "You did that on purpose!"

She put on her best look of innocence. "I don't know what you're talking about."

Now he leaned back in his chair and looked at Sarah. "So what did you mean about the girl in the zombie video?"

Sarah was clenching a wet washcloth against her

forearm where a laceration still continued to ooze blood. "The video we were talking with Eric about yesterday. The one Emily White posted before she disappeared."

David sipped his beer. "Yeah, I've never seen it."

Amy looked up from her leg. "You haven't?"

David shook his head. "Never knew how to find it."

"You got a computer?"

David slid his laptop over and the three of them gathered around it as it booted up. "Connection's kind of sketchy, so don't expect too much."

Sarah opened YouTube and found Emily's account, then searched for the video. "Here it is," she said. "It was definitely taken at the place we saw tonight."

They all watched as the footage blazed onto the screen. David studied the images, transfixed by what he saw.

"Looks like a lot of the same people that were there tonight," Amy said. "You know any of them?"

David shrugged. "I've seen a few of them in town. Don't really know them by name."

On the screen the masked man portraying Bacalou was dancing madly.

"Any idea who that is?" Sarah asked.

David shook his head. "Can't see his face. No marks or scars on his body. I've got no clue."

They continued to watch as Bacalou swiped the chicken across the girl's body, then ripped it open with the knife. Just at the moment when the girl opened her eyes and sat up, Sarah paused the video. "Now look. That's the same girl we saw tonight."

David squinted at the screen. "Maybe. Hard to tell. The video's not very clear."

"I tell you it's the same girl," Sarah said. "Look at

the shape of her face."

"Is she anyone you know, David?" Amy asked.

He shook his head. "Never seen her before."

Sarah closed out of YouTube and leaned back. She peeked beneath the washcloth at her wound and Amy noticed with alarm that her face was white. "I think I need to lie down," Sarah said.

Amy and David helped her over to the sofa. "Are you okay? Do we need to take you to the ER?"

"There's not one here," David said.

Amy gaped at him. "You're kidding. Look at her. She needs a doctor. Maybe stitches."

"There's a clinic in town," David said. "They have an emergency number. We can call and have someone meet us there."

Sarah raised her hand. "Guys, please, I'm all right. Blood just makes me. . . want to pass out. I'll be okay. Just let me stay here on the couch."

Amy knelt beside her. "You want something to drink? Some water?"

Sarah nodded. "Water would be great."

David grabbed a bottle out of the refrigerator and uncapped it for her. "You want a wine chaser with that?"

She laughed and took a sip from the bottle. "Water's fine. Thanks." She lay back and closed her eyes. "You guys go on and party without me. I'll be okay when the room stops spinning."

Amy brushed the sweaty hair off Sarah's forehead. "I'll be right here. If you start feeling worse. . ."

"I'll call for you," Sarah said. "I promise." She looked at David. "Put another record on. Something soft and slow."

"Got some Julie London?" Amy said.

"Sure do," David told her. He pulled an album from the shelf and placed it on the turntable.

Amy watched his fingers maneuver the record and marveled that the strong hands that had guided the boat and deftly tied off lines could be that gentle with something so delicate. She wondered, certainly not for the first time, how those hands would feel on her. Julie's smoky voice floated over the restrained guitar runs, and Amy felt the music move through her, stirring again those feelings she had so desperately attempted to push away.

David turned the light out beside the sofa and motioned back toward the kitchen. "Let's go out on the deck." He switched off the overhead light, leaving a small fluorescent burning above the sink, and grabbed his beer. "Want one of these?"

She shrugged. "Sure."

Outside, the air was sultry but not unpleasant. Amy sank into the patio chair and took a sip of beer. It was cold and felt delicious trickling down her throat. "So what do you do when you're not giving tours?"

"Not much," he said, taking a seat beside her. "I usually work six days a week. Seven during peak season."

"Wow," she said. "Don't you get tired?"

"Compared to my last job? Hardly. The physical labor is tough, but it's not draining like the mental work of banking. When I was in Indy I came home exhausted every night. Most days I put in ten hours. Sometimes I'd go in on weekends. The sad part is, no one really knew how hard I was working, or if they did, they didn't seem to care."

Amy sipped her beer. "That's shitty."

David nodded. "It was. Things were so monotonous, just the same reports, the same figures day after day, chasing everything down to the last penny all day long."

"So what made you decide to take the plunge and quit?"

He blew out a breath. "I'd been having panic attacks off and on for about a year. One Sunday afternoon I was working alone in the office and I started tingling all over. My lips went numb even. Felt like my chest was going to explode. I thought I was having a fucking heart attack. I left the bank and drove to the hospital – "

"Wait." Amy sat up. "You thought you were having a heart attack and you drove *yourself* to the hospital?"

He laughed. "I didn't say I was real smart guy." He ran his finger along the lip of the beer bottle. "Anyway, the ER doc told me it was just a panic attack. The worst I'd ever had. Said if I didn't get out from under the stress I'd likely have a heart attack for real one day."

"Wow."

"So I decided to take a couple of weeks off. I figured I'd get some rest, then go back to work and everything would be fine."

Amy looked at him. "So what happened?"

"Beth and I – "

"Beth?"

He pointed toward the kitchen. "The girl in the photo. We came down here to St. Celine. Fell in love with the place. Had a grand time. Left my phone in the suitcase. Never turned it on, in fact. Two weeks went by in a flash, and suddenly we were back in Indy and I was going to work on Monday morning, and everything just hit me again all at once. I realized I couldn't do it anymore. I had to get away from there."

"So you just quit?"

He nodded. "Gave my two weeks' notice that day. Beth and I had met Eric down here when we went fishing, and we really hit it off. He told me off the record the old man running the harbor tour was going to call it quits. Kind of made a joke about Beth and me moving down here and taking it over. Even gave me his phone number. I didn't think much about it at the time, but that day I when was taking the elevator up to my floor, my stomach was on fire and I had that awful, sinking feeling in my chest, and I decided I would do it."

Amy laughed. "Just like that? In the elevator?"

David smiled. "It was the first spontaneous thing I'd ever done in my life." He took a swig of beer. "The elevator doors opened, and instead of going to my office I headed down the hall to see my boss and tell him I was quitting."

Amy threw her head back. "I love it! What did he say?"

"They tried everything to keep me," David said. "Even offered me a ten-grand-a-year raise."

"That must have been hard to turn down."

David shook his head. "No, not really. See, I knew if I stayed, if I played their game, it was going to kill me. It wasn't about the money. It was about something else – getting my life back."

Amy looked at her beer. "So I take it Beth didn't share your enthusiasm."

He gave a dry laugh. "That's putting it mildly. It got really ugly. She told me I was ruining her life. *Her* life. And that I was killing her dreams. Those are the exact words she used: 'killing her dreams.' Like my sole purpose for living was to please her." He blew out a breath. "And you know what? Breaking it off with

Beth actually felt better than quitting my job. See, I finally realized what had been driving me all that time. It wasn't my own ambition. It was Beth's."

Amy looked at him. He was staring up at the stars. She reached out and took his hand. It was warm and dry, and he didn't pull away. She wondered how she would have felt about him if she had met him in his former life as a passionless banker, and she realized she wouldn't have given him a second glance. She knew that type – the kind that was wrapped up in themselves and their careers and had nothing left for anything else in life; after all, she had been married to one of them. She leaned over and kissed his stubbled cheek.

He looked at her in surprise, then put his hand in her hair and stroked it. She nuzzled against his arm and pulled his fingers to her mouth and kissed them. And suddenly his mouth was on hers and she was tasting him. Not the beer or the sweat, but *him*. She brushed her hand across his cropped hair, down along his cheek to his neck and pulled him closer. She wanted him. All of him. Her fingers found their way under his shirt and tangled themselves in the hair on his chest, brushed his nipples and felt them respond. He moaned and his tongue probed deeper into her mouth. Then his hand was sliding up her waist, cupping her breast, and all she could think was that she wanted her bra off, that she wanted his fingers touching her bare skin. That she wanted him inside her, that she wanted her body moving against his. Her hands traveled to his crotch and she felt him straining against his shorts. He pulled back and looked at her, and his eyes were dark and wanting.

Amy was aware of the sudden silence. "The record's over," she said.

"Is it?" he said, and his voice was husky.

She giggled. "Want to take this party someplace more comfortable?"

"Do you?"

She nodded. "I believe I do."

He followed her back into the house and closed the patio doors behind him. "I. . . I don't think I have any protection," he whispered. "I mean, I've got some, but they're kind of old, and I don't know. . . Do condoms expire?"

She turned and looked at him and couldn't help but smile. God, he was so cute and vulnerable. "Never fear," she said. "I'm always packing."

He blinked. "Oh. Okay."

"Let me get my bag. And I want to check on Sarah."

"Sure."

Amy grabbed her purse, then leaned over the back of the couch. Sarah's eyes were closed and she was breathing deeply. She stepped back into the kitchen. "She's asleep."

One moment he was looking into her eyes, and the next he was kissing her again. She put her arms around him and tugged his shirt up his back. He slipped out of it and flung it onto a chair. She bent over and flicked her tongue against one of his nipples and he let out a groan. He pulled away and took her by the hand, leading her down a short hallway into the bedroom. It was dark here, but she could see his eyes glistening with desire in the faint light from the kitchen. She pulled out of her t-shirt, hearing a couple of threads snap, and unhooked her bra. His mouth was on her at once, and she held his head to her as he teased her with his tongue.

She knelt, pulling the shorts down his legs at the same time. His hardness sprang up at her face and they both giggled. "Sorry about that," he said in a throaty whisper.

She stood and took him into her hands, feeling the heat of his erection. "That's certainly no little todger," she said with a smile.

16

Sarah awoke with a start, unsure for a moment where she was. Then she remembered. The ceremony. The sightless girl. The long trek back to David's house. The bloody cut on her arm and the feeling of seeing the room spin away. Had she passed out? She couldn't recall.

She'd hated the sight of blood since the accident. Since the moment Robert's Explorer had skidded on the November ice and slammed into the guardrail, the moment the rail plowed through the windshield and crushed Robert's chest. The moment she had been bathed in blood – Robert's and her own. The eternity she had spent pinned in her seat, watching the life in Robert's eyes ebb away and listening to the faint wail of sirens grow steadily louder. The moment she realized he had been taken away from her, and nothing would ever be the same again.

She rolled over onto her side. The room was dark

and quiet. She wondered what time it was, and how long she had been asleep. The cut on her arm throbbed and she examined it in the dim light from the kitchen. It had finally stopped bleeding and crusted over. She fought the urge to gag and sat up, rubbing her temples. Where were Amy and David?

She stood and made her way into the kitchen. She opened the patio door and peered out into the night. The deck was empty. A large furry shape darted inside and she nearly screamed until she realized it was just Seymour. He gave her a glance over his shoulder and flicked his tail, then sauntered into the dark hallway.

Sarah followed him, feeling her way in the darkness. "Amy?" she whispered. "Are you in here?"

Seymour disappeared behind a cracked door, and Sarah went after him. She placed her hand on the door and it swung open easily.

David lay on the bed in the faint light, snoring. He was shirtless, and the sheets were tangled around his waist and legs. Amy was snuggled next to him, her head on his chest. Seymour hopped onto the bed, regarded her for a moment, and began to bathe.

Sarah backed slowly out of the room, pulling the door shut as she did so. Her face was hot. She felt sickened. Why, she didn't know. It had been inevitable from the moment Amy first met him. Sarah had expected them to end up in bed together sooner or later, but she never expected to find out about it like this.

In the kitchen she pulled a Coke from the refrigerator and slipped through the patio doors to the deck. The black sky was speckled with glistening stars of a clarity she'd never seen in the city. She eased into one of the chairs and leaned her head back, staring into the vastness. Was Heaven out there somewhere? Was God watching her at this very moment? Was Robert there?

The stars blurred and she realized tears were spilling down her face. It wasn't fair. She had only ever loved one man in her life. Just one. And he had been ripped from her in one senseless moment. And Amy seemed content to bed down with anyone, whether she loved them or not. Whether it was moral or not. What did it matter, trying to stay clean and pure when the disparate concepts of good and sinful seemed to have no bearing on the outcome? When there was neither punishment nor reward – just circumstances? She wiped her eyes with the heel of her hand and took a deep breath. It was no use questioning God. It only led to frustration and disappointment.

She touched her lips to the soda can and stopped. She could hear drums in the distance. The ceremony was still going on. But something was different. The drums sounded more urgent. Frenzied. She felt her pulse quicken until her heartbeat matched the cadence of the drums beat for beat. The pounding was in her head, throughout her body. She felt herself swaying with the rhythm, becoming part of it.

The drums were calling her. She knew it as surely as if something had called her name. She had to go to them. She *must* go. She stood and the soda can fell to the deck with a thunk.

What was she doing? Had she actually considered going back to the ceremony? What was wrong with her? She reached down to grab the spilled soda and stopped.

Someone was standing off to the side of the deck. She could see the form silhouetted beside the corner of the house. This time she knew it was no worker from the inn. It wasn't another vision of Robert. It wasn't

David or Amy. "Who's there?" she said.

The figure didn't move.

She looked back toward the kitchen. David had left his flashlight on the table. She could see it lying beside the opened bag of cotton balls.

Keeping her eyes on the shape, she reached for the patio door and slid it open. The table was just steps away. She entered the doorway and grabbed the flashlight in a single movement, then emerged back onto the deck. She fully expected the figure to be gone. It wasn't. She flicked on the light.

It was the little girl from the ceremony. Her white eyes stared blankly ahead. No. Not blankly. They appeared to be looking straight at Sarah.

She wanted to scream. Her mouth opened, but no sound came out. She continued to stare at the girl. "What do you want?" she managed to croak.

The girl raised her upturned hand, beckoning Sarah to follow her.

Sarah felt a wave of horror. "No," she whispered.

The girl motioned for Sarah again. The drums continued to hammer in the distance.

"No," Sarah said again, more insistent. "Leave me alone." She couldn't stop staring into those milky sightless eyes. She took a step forward. It was as if she were being pulled. She moved closer to the steps.

She should yell for Amy and David. Why couldn't she scream? Her throat seemed constricted, closed off.

Why wouldn't those damned drums *stop*? She covered her ears, trying to muffle the noise, but the pounding continued. It was inside her head. She could feel it pulsing in her ears.

The girl beckoned again.

This time Sarah made her way down the steps to the

sparse grass of the yard.

The girl turned and disappeared around the corner of the house.

Sarah followed.

The girl trudged up the road, back toward the clearing, back toward the relentless drums. Sarah trailed behind, keeping the flashlight on the girl's faded gingham dress, watching her bare feet as they plodded tirelessly along. The drums grew louder as they reached the dirt lane, and Sarah could see the glow from the pavilion through the trees.

This wasn't right. The people would see her. They would know she was there. Would know she had seen. And Amy wasn't with her. David wasn't with her to smooth things over with them. She had to stop. She had to turn back.

But she couldn't. The drums kept pulling her forward, ever closer to the bonfire and the singing congregation. She could see them now, swaying and dancing in rhythm with the drums.

The girl continued to move forward. They were almost at the end of the lane, threading between the collection of cars and bicycles parked haphazardly in the clearing. Any moment now, someone would spot them. Someone would see her and she would be grabbed and questioned. And what was she going to say? How could she explain herself? Her heart pounded in time with the drums. Her whole body was vibrating, throbbing, pulsating.

The girl stopped at the edge of the clearing.

Sarah was in full view of them now. They were looking at her. All of them. They continued to chant and sing and dance, and the drums pounded on endlessly.

Mama Alice stepped forward, shaking a rattle and singing along with the others.

"I'm sorry, Mama Alice," Sarah cried. She could feel hot tears coursing down her cheeks. Her words were drowned out by the cacophony. She held out her hands, pleading. The flashlight fell to the ground.

Mama Alice took her hand and gently led her toward the circle.

She didn't understand. They didn't seem to be upset that she was there. They seemed. . . *glad*. Almost as if they had been expecting her.

Mama Alice thrust a cup into her hands. "Don't be afraid, child," she said above the din. "Drink this. It'll help you relax."

"What is it?"

"Tea. A special blend."

Sarah sniffed at the concoction. It smelled strong and sour. She took a sip. It was hot and tart, and she felt her lips pucker. She laughed. It was almost like hot lemonade. She took another drink.

"That's right, child," Mama Alice said. "Drink it all up."

Sarah tilted the cup up, drinking every last drop. It was warm and felt good in her stomach. She was laughing again. She couldn't seem to stop. She turned to look at Mama Alice and the world tilted sideways. She couldn't stand upright. "What's happening?"

Half a dozen stout arms held onto her and eased her down to the ground. Something was pressed onto her head. She reached up and felt a ringlet of flowers. She could smell them, sweet and pungent.

The people around her continued to gyrate and sing. The rhythm of the drums quickened to a frenzy. Or was that in her mind? She couldn't tell. She was so dizzy.

So sleepy. If she could just close her eyes for a while. If she could just sleep.

She jolted awake. Mama Alice had given her something. Something in the tea. "*No!*" She tried to rise, but her arms and legs had no strength. She fell back against the ground. "What did you give me!"

In the blur of faces around her, one stood out. It moved closer. It was Marko, the shuttle driver from the inn. He was dancing with the others. He was shirtless, and his muscular chest glistened with sweat.

"Marko! Oh, thank God!" She tried to reach for him, but her arms stayed limp at her sides. "They gave me something! I can't move!"

He danced closer to her, his hips moving suggestively, seductively.

"Marko!"

From behind, hands lowered a mask over his face. It was painted with a red skull.

Sarah screamed, but her voice was drowned out by the deafening roar of the drums.

III

THE CULT
OF BACALOU

D avid awoke in the morning light and felt Amy's warmth beside him. A smile played across his lips as he remembered the night before, remembered everything they had done together. She had seduced him. God almighty if she hadn't. She'd taken control and driven him right over the edge. And he had happily let her do it. She was so free and uninhibited. Nothing like Beth, who had hardly ever moved when they made love.

This had been his first time since coming to the island, and he had just about decided to opt for a life of celibacy. The girls on St. Celine held no interest for him. Beautiful as many of them were, they were uneducated and backward and seemed content to let a man take care of them. He hated that. He had seen that trait in his own mother, watched how his father took the lead in everything and made all the decisions while she followed blithely along like a child. He supposed that was why he had first been attracted to Beth; she was strong-willed and not afraid to voice her own opinion. But Beth was controlling. He could see that now; he sure didn't want to get mixed up in that again. And he had made the conscious decision to keep tourists at arms' length. He knew plenty of guys would have taken the opportunity to bag the many giggly, silly, drunken women that crossed his path, and back in college he wouldn't have said no to an occasional casual lay. But those days were behind him. He was looking for something real now, something that would last. A real relationship. He just hoped he hadn't made a mistake last night.

Amy stirred against him and opened her eyes. She smiled. "Hello, handsome."

He kissed her on the forehead. "Good morning."

She gave a contented sigh and ran a hand across his chest. "You snore."

"Do I?" Beth had never told him that, and he wondered if the extra weight he was now carrying had something to do with it. "Sorry."

"It's okay. I've heard worse."

He brushed his fingers through her hair. "I want you to know, I'm not in the habit of doing this."

She looked up at him. "What? Snoring?"

"Picking up tourists for a roll in the hay."

"I see."

"In fact, you're the first woman to share my bed since I came down here."

"Is that supposed to make me feel privileged," she said, "or am I supposed to feel like I took the last cookie from the jar?"

"Neither," he said quickly. "I'm just saying you're the first woman to turn my head in a long time. Intelligent, beautiful. . ."

She smiled. "Keep going."

"Witty. Crazy."

"Go back to intelligent and beautiful."

"I really enjoyed last night. Not just. . . you know, but everything. Dinner. Running through the dark scared shitless."

She giggled. "It *was* fun." She propped herself up on an elbow. "Thanks for going with us."

"Thanks for asking me."

"I don't know what we would've done if you hadn't been there to get us back to the road. Sarah would've been hysterical. I probably would've panicked and gotten us lost."

"You would've been okay."

She ran a finger in a circle around his nipple. "Why don't you let me fix breakfast for all of us? Show you my appreciation."

"Probably not much to choose from in there," he said. "Bread for toast, if it hasn't molded. I may have a few eggs. No bacon."

"Well, maybe we could go out to one of the cafés in town."

"That's more like it."

She sat up, keeping the sheet wrapped around her breasts and fumbled for her clothes on the floor beside the bed.

"Why do women do that?" he said.

"Do what?"

"You're all so self-conscious about your bodies in the morning. It's not like I didn't see it all last night."

She turned her back to him and let the sheet fall as she slipped on her bra. "Because in the daylight you can see all our imperfections. The dark hides a lot."

He leaned up on the pillow, watching her dress. Strangely, it was almost as arousing watching the clothes go on as it had been when they came off. "You've got nothing to be ashamed of," he said. He looked down at his belly. "I, on the other hand. . ."

She turned and looked at him as she stepped into her panties. "You're just fine," she said. "I like my men big and burly."

"I'm *burly*?"

"You're perfect," she said. She pulled her t-shirt over her head. "I'm going to check on Sarah."

He watched her leave, then sank back into the bed. He couldn't help but smile. He had never felt less attractive in his life, but now a beautiful young woman had just told him he was perfect. Even if she was just shitting him, it still felt good.

"David!"

He sat up immediately. "What is it?"

Amy appeared at the bedroom door. "Sarah's gone!"

"Are you sure? Did you check the deck?"

"I checked. She's not here."

"You think she went back to the inn?"

"The golf cart's still here."

He swung out of the bed and pulled on his shorts. "Maybe she walked."

"Why would she do that?"

He followed Amy back to the kitchen, peering out the patio doors. A Coke lay on its side on the deck. Its contents had spilled, staining the wood. There was no sign of Sarah.

Amy was digging into her bag. "I'm calling her cell."

"You know it's expensive to use those things down here."

She had her phone out and was punching in Sarah's number. "I don't care, it's an emergency."

They stood frozen while the call connected. And suddenly tinny music rang out. Benny Goodman's "Sing, Sing, Sing." They followed the noise to the living room. Sarah's phone was in her purse, next to the sofa.

"She's got to be around here somewhere then," David said. "Let's check outside."

The morning air was damp and chilly, and David wished he'd put on a shirt. He hoped they would find her sitting on the front steps or wandering around in the yard, but there was nothing. The golf cart sat where they had parked it the night before, right next to David's Honda. Amy called out to Sarah several times, but the only answer was the chattering of birds in the trees.

"I'm going back to the inn," Amy said, stomping up the steps to the house. "She must have gone back there."

A new thought struck him. "Do you think she. . . knew about us and got mad?"

"I guess anything's possible," Amy said. She grabbed Sarah's bag and her own. "You coming with me?"

"Of course," he said. "Let me grab a shirt."

2

Amy's stomach burned as she guided the golf cart along the road, dodging potholes and swerving around the deeper ruts. She was sick – half with worry and half with anger that Sarah might have just wandered off by herself without telling anyone. What was she thinking? Her damned obsession with Josh and Emily White should have been enough to scare her into staying put for the night. What would she do if Sarah wasn't at the inn? The next step would be to contact the police, and she was glad David was along to help her. She couldn't imagine trying to navigate all this on her own.

David followed behind her on his Honda. His comment that Sarah might have known they were in bed together and left in a huff, crazy as it sounded, had a ring of truth to it. She knew Sarah wouldn't approve of her sleeping with David so soon, and it would be just like her to try to punish Amy in some passive-aggressive way like heading back to the hotel without telling them, just so they would worry. But why wouldn't she have taken the cart? And why would she have left her purse behind?

She slowed as they entered the town, and she scanned the tourists meandering the sidewalks on the strip. It was still early and few people were out and about, which made it easy to look for Sarah among them. But if she were in town, she could be in any of the shops or cafés. She took a deep breath. The sensible thing would be to check the inn first, then take it from there.

On the hill, she pulled into one of the spots reserved for golf carts and waited for David to park his motorcycle and catch up with her. The sight of him heading toward her across the parking lot was comforting, and she felt a sense of calm, a feeling that everything would be okay. He followed her through the lobby and up the stairs to the room, and his presence quieted the panic that had begun to creep into her.

Her hands were shaking as she unlocked the door. "Sarah?"

Sarah lay on top of her bed in the darkened room, still in her clothes. She sat up abruptly. "What's wrong?"

Amy fumbled for the light switch, and the glare of the lamp flooded the room. "Where in the fuck have you been?"

Sarah looked at her, then at David behind. "What do you mean?"

"Why did you leave David's?"

Sarah shook her head, her eyes confused. She looked around the room. "I. . . I don't know."

"I was worried sick," Amy said. "What did you do,

walk back here in the dark?"

Sarah brushed the tousled hair back from her face. "I don't remember."

Amy's relief gave way to irritation. "What do you mean, you don't remember?" She held up Sarah's purse. "Your hotel key's still in here. Did you have somebody at the front desk let you in?"

Sarah shook her head, her eyes growing round and frightened. "I don't know." She rubbed her temples. "I don't remember coming back here."

Amy sat down beside her on the bed. "Are you all right? What's the last thing you do remember?"

Sarah looked back and forth between Amy and David. "I. . . remember lying down on the couch. I remember listening to Julie London. I remember hearing you guys go out onto the deck." She stopped, staring straight ahead. "That's all."

Amy put a hand on Sarah's shoulder. "You're telling me you have no idea how you got back here to the room?"

Sarah shook her head. She rubbed her eyes with her fingertips. "I'm so thirsty."

Amy glanced at David. "Get her some water."

David stepped into the bathroom and ran a glass of tap water, then handed it to Sarah. "How do you feel?"

Sarah took a sip from the glass. "Just. . . sleepy. Tired."

David looked at Amy. "I wonder if the blood loss from that bad cut made her confused."

Amy pulled a strand of hair from Sarah's face. "I think we need to get you to a doctor," she told her.

Sarah shook her head. "No, I'm all right." She showed them her arm, where the cut had scabbed over. "See? It's better."

Amy ran a fingertip over it gingerly. "Still," she said, "it might not hurt to get you checked out. What if you get an infection?"

Sarah swallowed a gulp of water. "I think you put enough alcohol on it to kill anything that might have been lurking around on it." She grabbed Amy's hand. "I'm fine. Really. I must have been sleepwalking or something. We had such a busy day yesterday, and I must have been so tired when I got back here that I just don't remember asking someone to let me into the room."

Amy met Sarah's gaze. "You're sure you're all right?"

Sarah nodded. "Yeah. I'm okay. Sorry I made you guys worry." She looked down at herself. "I would like to get a shower, though. I feel really nasty."

Amy was aware of her own state. "Yeah, I wouldn't mind a good shower myself." She looked at David. "Raincheck on breakfast?"

"Sure," he said, but she could see disappointment in his eyes.

She grabbed his hand. "Maybe we could do lunch?"

He nodded. "Yeah, I'd like that. How about we meet in front of Jolly Roger's around noon?"

"Sounds good." She followed him to the door.

He turned and looked at her, and she wondered if he would move to kiss her. He glanced at Sarah, then back at Amy. "I'll see you then."

She closed the door behind him and leaned against it. Sarah was looking at her. "What?"

"You slept with him, didn't you?"

Amy blew out a breath. "Look, Sarah, don't get all judgmental with me."

Sarah climbed off the bed and rooted through her

fresh underwear in the dresser drawer. "I'm not being judgmental," she said. "I'm just questioning the wisdom of hopping into bed with someone you just met."

"He's a nice guy, Sarah. He's great to talk to, easygoing." She stopped and sank back onto the bed. "You don't understand. I *need* a nice guy. I've been involved with so many losers."

Sarah turned and looked at her. "A nice guy whose heart you're going to break when we leave here." She frowned. "I see the way he looks at you. I think he's really fallen for you, Amy. It's not fair to him. It's not right to string him along." She disappeared into the bathroom and shut the door behind her.

Amy sat staring at the closed door. Sarah was right, of course. But was she really stringing David along? Surely he knew there was no chance of anything longterm in what they had enjoyed last night. At the end of the week she and Sarah would head back to Cedar Hill, and he would go back to his humdrum island life. It was inevitable. There was no possibility of having a future together.

She lay back on the bed. The thing was, she didn't want it to end. There was something about him she'd never seen in another man. A kindness. A vulnerability. A focus on life besides chasing what the world saw as success. And she knew she would never find it with anyone else she might meet in the future. What if he was The One, her soul mate? What if she left St. Celine and never saw him again? She didn't think she could bear that.

She stared at the ceiling and felt tears seep from her eyes. Sarah was right – David had fallen for her, but she had fallen for him, too. It just wasn't fair.

3

Sarah started the bathwater and felt it grow warmer as it cascaded over her fingers. She wondered if she had ticked Amy off with what she'd said, but she decided it didn't matter. She had a fleeting memory of seeing the two of them in bed together, but she wasn't sure where it fit in with what little she could recall from last night. Was it before or after she had fallen asleep on David's sofa? And had she really seen it, or was it part of some dream?

She had tried not to show it, but she was terrified when she thought of a whole chunk of time missing from her memory. What had happened? Had she really walked all the way from David's house back to the inn in the middle of the night? Had she been so exhausted that she'd not been fully awake and stumbled the distance down David's road, all the way through town, and up the hill to the inn and couldn't remember one single detail of the journey? She found it hard to believe, and yet she had no other explanation.

She wondered, not for the first time, about her sanity. After all, she had hallucinated Robert, had imagined all kinds of things back in Cedar Hill. Maybe this was just the latest episode in a deteriorating mental condition. What would she do if it got worse? What if she got to the point where she could no longer teach? She couldn't be a burden to her parents. She couldn't allow them to put aside everything and take care of her.

The water was hot. She turned on the shower and began peeling off her clothes. They seemed stuck to her, and it would feel good to scrub herself clean.

God, she was sore. She looked at her abdomen and felt a sting of shock. She was covered in bruises. Not just there. Her arms and her shins were also discolored in spots. Surely that wasn't just the results of running haphazardly through the forest. What the hell had she done last night? Had she fallen? Had she been attacked?

She turned to step into the shower and something caught her eye in the mirror. Something red on her right buttock. She stared at it, trying to comprehend what she was seeing.

A crude skull and crossbones was drawn on her skin. She reached her trembling fingers around and touched it. It smeared. She opened her mouth to call to Amy, then decided against it. She didn't need Amy freaking out right now. Amy would have questions, and Sarah knew she couldn't answer them. She rubbed the drawing, obliterating it into a big red stain.

Fear coursed through her like ice in her veins. She hadn't come straight to the inn. Something else had happened.

She went through the events in her mind. Having

dinner at David's. Walking up the road toward the activity in the pavilion. Watching the ceremony. Seeing the little girl with the milky white eyes. Running through the brush and back down the road. Being back at David's and feeling like she would pass out. Then nothing after that.

The girl with the milky eyes.

There was something else about the girl with the white eyes. What was it? Had she dreamed about her? Why couldn't she remember?

She stared at the red smudge until the steam from the shower covered the mirror.

4

When he spotted Amy through the crowd, he felt his heart leap. At the same time, he recognized the futility of it. There was no doubt he had fallen head over heels for her, and it angered him that he'd allowed himself to get to this point. Especially so quickly. And knowing how it was all going to end. But he refused to allow himself to think about that now. He deserved some happiness, damn it, even if it was only for a short while.

"Hey," she said, kissing him on the cheek.

He looked behind her. "Where's Sarah?"

She shrugged. "At the inn. Said she was going to stay by the pool. I think she's still tired. I'm worried about her. That whole episode last night? I mean, what the fuck?"

"I know," he said, pulling her in the door of Jolly Roger's. He led her to a table in a dark corner and they took their seats. "Has she had any. . . problems in the past?"

Amy shook her head. "Not really. I mean, I know she had a tough time after the accident. And right before we came down she told me she thought she'd seen Robert."

"*Seen* him?"

"Yeah. Like a hallucination. But I've never known her to do anything as off the wall as what she did last night."

Chelsea, one of the regular waitresses, brought their menus and gave David a knowing wink. "Hey, Todger," she said, and his face burned like fire.

"Hey," he said, taking his menu and not meeting her eyes.

Like him, Chelsea was a transplanted American. She had also first come to St. Celine on a vacation, but she fell in love with a fisherman, a native islander, and had stayed on and married him. She and David often had long conversations, sometimes up until closing time. At first he wondered if maybe she was flirting with him, but as he got to know her, he realized she was just being friendly. She adored her husband and their daughter and often showed him pictures.

Amy leaned in close. "Should I tell her the rumor isn't true?"

If possible, his face burned even hotter and he focused on the menu in front of him, but he couldn't help but smile. He cleared his throat. "You think maybe the car accident might have affected Sarah's brain?"

Amy shook her head. "I don't think so. She didn't seem to have any trouble getting back to her classes. I actually think it was good for her to get back to work. To get her mind off everything."

"What exactly happened?"

"I'm not a hundred percent sure, but I know they hit a patch of ice and struck a guardrail. Robert died almost instantly. Sarah was trapped until help arrived. A couple of hours, I think."

"Wow."

"She doesn't like to talk about it."

"I guess not."

"Anyway, that was one of the reasons I wanted to bring her on this trip. She needed to get away, to stop brooding in that big old house of hers and start living again. I figured a trip to the Bahamas would do the trick."

He smiled at her. "You're a good friend."

"I try." She was tearing at the paper wrapper around her straw. He reached out and took her hand. She held onto him, keeping her gaze on the table. "I don't want this week to end," she said.

Something inside him melted. "I don't either."

"I mean, I never expected anything like this." She looked at him. "All I was wanting was a few days in the sun, lying on the beach and drinking margaritas. Maybe doing a little shopping with Sarah. I had no idea I would. . ."

"I know," he said. He watched their fingers intertwine. "So where do we go from here?"

"I'm not sure," Amy said. "Fuck, this is hard." She gave a sniff, and David realized she was blinking back tears. "I don't want this to be over once I get back on that ferry," she said. "I don't want to go back home and never see you again. You're the first decent guy I've met in a long time. I guess that's why I'm having such a hard time with this. I don't want to hurt you."

He squeezed her hand. "I don't want to hurt you, either." He shifted in his seat. "Look, I meant what I said this morning. I haven't been with anyone since I left Beth. I'm not one of those guys that hops into bed with a woman on a whim."

"I know you're not."

"I have to feel a real connection with someone."

"I understand."

"I guess what I'm saying is, I feel that connection with you. And I haven't felt that in years."

Tears coursed down Amy's cheeks. "I'm the same way. I'd just about given up on ever finding anyone worthwhile." She looked into his eyes. "I don't want to lose you."

"I don't want to lose you, either." He took a deep breath. "So. . . back to the question. What do we do?"

"You guys ready to order?" Chelsea said, popping up beside them.

David smiled up at her. "How about a big platter of answers?"

5

After lunch, Amy followed David across the street to the marina so he could check on the *New Beginning*. She was relieved to see Eric's boat out of the slip. Friendly as he was, she didn't want to give up this opportunity to have David all to herself. She climbed to the sun deck atop the boat and stared out at the harbor as David busied himself below, checking lines and whatever else he was doing. Boats and yachts came and went, and she followed the ferry as it made its way into port and docked at the far end of the marina and disgorged its fresh load of tourists.

So David felt the same way about her. While she couldn't help but be thrilled, part of her knew it would make their parting all the more painful. What was she going to do when she finally had to tell him goodbye? What would *he* do?

He couldn't very well follow her home. His place

was here, on the island. His business was here. His new life was here. What kind of existence could he hope for, living in Cedar Hill and choking on society and academia? There was always the lake west of the city. And while the demand for tours of an inland lake couldn't rival that of a Bahamian island, it might be something.

Who was she kidding? David would no more move back to the states than fly to the moon. He would end up back in the corporate world. Or worse, back in banking. And he would be completely miserable. It was, after all, the very thing he had moved here to escape. She couldn't ask him to go back to that.

But then there was another possibility. What if she moved to St. Celine? What if she did what David had done and chucked it all to live out the rest of her days on the island? Could she stand it? Would she be happy here, with no culture, no arts scene, no entertainment to speak of? What could she do, work in a shop? Help David on the boat tours? It was an endless stream of questions with no answers. Moving here was not the solution either. She had no idea what would happen when Sunday came and she had to tell him goodbye. She forced herself to concentrate on the vivid blue water of the harbor and not think about going back home.

"You still awake?"

She looked to see David on the ladder to the sun deck, his head poking just above the floor. "Enjoying the view," she said.

He climbed up and took a seat on the lounge next to her. "Here," he said, handing her a bottle of Dasani. "Figured you could use this."

"Thanks." She took a sip and let the cold wash down her throat. She hadn't realized how thirsty she had become up here in the sun.

"Radio says there's a tropical storm brewing off to the east. First one of the year."

"Is that bad?"

"Don't know yet. Depends on which way it moves."

"You been through a hurricane?"

He nodded. "Sandy. Did some major damage on Grand Bahama, but we were lucky here." He followed her gaze out across the harbor. "Nice, isn't it?"

"I see why you fell in love with the place."

He slipped off his sunglasses and looked at her. "You know, my bungalow's big enough for two."

A thrill shot through her, followed immediately by the cold weight of reality. "David. . ."

"I'm just sayin'."

She took a deep breath. "You know that's what I've been sitting up here thinking about."

"It is?"

"David, I don't know that I could live here. What would I do?"

"You could help me run the tour business."

"I don't know the first thing about boats."

"I can teach you."

"Or business."

"I could teach you that, too." He leaned in closer to her. "Look, I know we've only known each other a couple of days. I know this is crazy, but it's not half as messed up as it sounds. People do crazier shit every day. I like you. A lot."

She looked at him. "What are you saying?"

His ruddy face turned even redder. "I'm saying I think I may be in love with you. I'm saying that if you feel the same way about me, there may be a way we can make it work."

A warmth spread through her that had nothing to do with the heat of the sun. It was a mixture of joy and panic. It really was crazy, what he was suggesting. "David, I don't know. . ."

He put a finger to her lips. "Don't say anything else. Just think about it." He perched the sunglasses back on his face and looked out toward the sea. "You and I could really be happy here, Amy. Really happy."

Above them, a lone gull soared through the sky, riding the wind.

6

Sarah could not remember the last time she'd been
this drunk.

She came out to the pool right after Amy left, and
when the hotel waiter appeared at her side, she ordered
a piña colada, and when it was drained she promptly
ordered another. Now she was on her third. She'd
skipped lunch, and now her head swam. When the
waiter returned she would have to order a sandwich
from the grill. This was why she never drank to excess.
She'd be lucky to make it back to the room without falling up the stairs.

She reached for the sunscreen and caught sight of
Amy emerging from the door to the lobby. She was
smiling and waving. Sarah sprayed the sunscreen onto
her legs and began to rub it in. "How was lunch?"

"Great." Amy flopped down on the lounge chair beside her. "You should have come with me."

"And spoil your date? Don't be ridiculous."

Amy sighed. "Come on, Sarah, don't be like that."

She realized she was sounding like a bitch. "Sorry. I'm still so tired."

Amy pointed to her drink. "How many of those have you had?"

Sarah held up three fingers.

Amy gaped at her. "Have you eaten anything?"

"No. I thought I'd get a sandwich."

"You need food," Amy said. She waved her arm and the smiling waiter appeared out of nowhere. "Can we get something from the grill? A tuna sandwich and chips? And a coke?"

He nodded. "Certainly, miss."

"Send it up to 204."

"Absolutely." He gave a slight bow and was gone.

Sarah bit her lip. "I don't want to go back to the room."

"You need to get out of the sun. Come on." Amy took Sarah's hand and tugged her off the lounge. Suddenly she gasped. "What happened to your legs? Is that from last night?"

Sarah looked down at the bruises that mottled her thighs. "Yeah. I mean, I guess so." She was grateful the bathing suit covered the other marks on her back and abdomen.

"Wow, you really got banged up."

"Yeah." She swung her legs off the chair as she sat up. The world swam and she lay back down.

"You okay?"

"Dizzy."

"You're drunk."

Sarah giggled. "Yeah, I guess I am." Amy pulled her to her feet, and she could feel herself swaying. She leaned against her as they headed toward the doors of the inn. "How do you do it, Amy?"

"Do what?"

"Get three thousand miles away from home and end up fucking some guy you just met?"

Amy stiffened. "Sarah. . ."

"No, I mean it. What's your secret? Do you have some kind of magical power?"

Amy's grip tightened on Sarah's arm. "Stop it."

She could hear the irritation in Amy's voice and a thrill shot through her. "Or is your desire to fuck so strong that you just abandon your friend and go at it?"

Amy was shaking her head. "Shut up, Sarah."

"This was supposed to be *our trip*, Amy. Just you and me. We were supposed to be having fun. Together. It's like you can't go *anywhere* without jumping some random guy."

Amy stopped and swung Sarah around to look into her face. "Sarah, stop it. You're drunk. Don't say something you're going to regret later."

Sarah could tell she had struck a nerve. "Fine," she said, moving toward the door. "But there's more to life than fucking, Amy."

Behind her, Amy blew out a breath and followed her into the lobby.

7

Amy sat in the rocker on the balcony and watched the sky above the water turn a deep maroon as the sun sank below the horizon. It had been a couple of years since she'd smoked weed, but she could sure use a joint about now.

Behind her in the darkened room, Sarah was snoring in her bed. Asleep or passed out, Amy wasn't sure. It had taken some doing getting Sarah to the room, like trying to haul a hundred-pound sack of flour up the stairs. Once inside, she'd helped Sarah out of her bathing suit and into shorts and a t-shirt. She'd been shocked at all the bruises on Sarah's body. Had she fallen or something during their flight from the ceremony? Or had it happened during that period she couldn't account for? In any event, she didn't have time to question it because as soon as Sarah was dressed she doubled over and vomited into the toilet. Amy had seen her fair share of drunks, so she kept Sarah poised over the commode until she was sure nothing more was coming up. By the time Amy washed off her face and helped her to the bed, Sarah was crying. "I'm sorry, Amy," she said. "You're such a good friend. I'm so sorry I said all those awful things." And when the food arrived, she ate half the sandwich and drank the Coke before she was nodding off. Amy pulled the blanket over her, then finished off the sandwich and chips while sitting on the edge of the bed staring into space.

She took a nap herself and awoke with a fuzzy head when she heard a man and a woman arguing in the hall as they headed downstairs. She sat up and looked at the clock, surprised to see it was after seven and the light in the room was soft and pink. Sarah was still snoozing in the other bed, sleeping the thick, deep sleep of drunkards. The room was hot and stuffy. Amy opened the doors to the balcony and the sea breeze flowed in, salty and cool. She took a seat in one of the rockers, and she had been here ever since.

She still had no idea what she would do come Sunday. The thought of getting on that ferry and leaving David behind filled her with panic. She and David had decided to take a break tonight, as difficult as it was to stay apart, but Amy knew she needed some time away from him to clear her head. At lunch they had discussed their options, and none of them were very good. David didn't ruled out the possibility of moving back to the States at some point in the future, but Amy refused to let him do that for her sake. And David was adamant that Amy not give up the job she loved to move to the island just to be with him. It seemed they had reached a stalemate. Only one thing was certain, and that was their overwhelming attraction to each other. And it was more than just lust. She knew it. David had touched part of her soul that no other man had come near, not even Tim. It wasn't just physical; he had rooted himself into the part of her that was raw emotion, a part she had always kept locked away.

Dusk gave way to evening, and evening to night, and still she sat. The wind grew stronger and warmer, and she knew it was from the coming storm. It wasn't big enough to have a name yet, but Amy couldn't help feeling frightened. Growing up in Texas, she had experienced more than her fair share of tornadoes and straight-line winds, knew the damage they could bring, the destruction. A twister had devastated part of her hometown when she was seventeen, and she had been terrified of storms ever since. But this was nothing to worry about. David had said so, and she trusted him.

She realized that was what made David different. The trust. She hadn't trusted anyone since Tim. She hadn't wanted to take the chance.

At ten she decided there was no reason to stay up. She was making herself miserable and she wasn't coming up with any solutions. She was hungry, but the dining room had long since closed, and nothing on the room service menu looked appetizing. She got ready for bed and climbed under the covers, doused the light and stared at the darkness of the ceiling, waiting for sleep to come.

At some point, she must have dozed off because something pulled her back into consciousness, and she lay there listening and not opening her eyes. Drums. Far off in the distance. Another ceremony had to be going on. She rolled over onto her back. She hadn't expected to hear the drums from that far away. She opened her eyes and saw movement in the darkened room. She sat up, her heart in her throat.

Sarah was standing at the balcony doors, staring out into the night.

"You scared the shit out of me," Amy whispered. "What are you doing?"

Sarah didn't answer. She moved out to the edge of the verandah and leaned against the rail. The wind caught her hair and whipped it around her face.

"Sarah?" Amy slipped from the bed and made her way through the darkness to the balcony. "Answer me."

Sarah's eyes were glazed and unfocused, and Amy realized she was sleepwalking. Is this what had happened at David's? She ran everything she knew about sleepwalking through her mind – don't make any sudden movements, don't try to wake the sleepwalker, steer her back to bed. . .

She took hold of Sarah's arm and tugged her toward the room. "Let's go back to bed."

Sarah stared into the darkness. She cocked her head as if listening to the drums pounding away. "Bacalou," she whispered.

Amy froze. Wasn't that the name of the *loa* Mama Alice's group supposedly worshipped? The bad one? She pulled harder at Sarah's arm. "Come on."

"Bacalou," Sarah whispered again. This time she stretched out her hand toward the sound of the relentless drums. "Bacalou."

Amy took a deep breath. This was starting to freak her out. "Sarah, come back to bed." She took hold of Sarah's shoulders and turned her back toward the room. This time Sarah did as she was told, shuffling along like an old woman. She reached the bed and crawled into it without any further protest. Amy pulled the covers up to Sarah's chin and felt herself relax as Sarah began to lightly snore.

Amy returned to the balcony doors. She could bare-ly hear the drums now for the wind through the trees. One of the lanterns in the courtyard below swayed from its hook, and the pattern from the light splashed about the palms and hibiscus like a kaleidoscope. She moved to close the doors and her blood became ice.

The man was back, standing in the shadows. She could see the full figure – head, arms and legs – silhou-etted against the clapboards of the inn. And this time she could tell he was watching her. His eyes were tiny pinpricks of light in the darkness.

She slammed the doors to and locked them, then felt her way through the room to the door on the far side. It was double-bolted and chained.

For a crazy moment, she thought of climbing into bed with Sarah, but then decided that was silly. They were safe in the room. No one could get in. The phone was on the table between the beds, and she could call hotel security in an instant. Her cellphone lay beside it, and she almost reached for it to call David.

She stopped herself. She was just psyching herself out. She had to calm down. The best thing she could do was get back into bed and go to sleep. And tomor-row, she would report the creepy bastard to the front desk.

But she wasn't sleeping with the windows open an-other night.

8

With the storm expected to hit, many of the smaller fishing boats were being moved from the marina. The wind and waves could shatter the smaller vessels, and their owners had chosen to lash them to trailers and frames inland rather than let them be dashed to pieces in the harbor. David and Eric did not have that option. For large boats like theirs, the only choice was to ride out the storm in the marina. All they could do was double their ties with storm lines, suspend fenders to protect the hulls from crashing into the dock or each other, and make sure the batteries were charged on their bilge pumps. For the past two years they had helped each other with these preparations. The first time it had taken them all day and into the evening, mostly because David had no idea what he was doing. Now both vessels could be secured by mid-afternoon.

From his self-storage unit at the marina office, he

grabbed his plywood to cover the engine vents and made his way down the dock to his boat slip. The wind caught the wood and nearly knocked him into the water, but he was able to keep his footing. Eric was already aboard the *Sundancer* covering his instruments with plastic and duct tape. "Hey there," David called to him.

Eric looked down from the bridge. "Hello, Todger. I think we may get some rain."

David laughed and looked at the sky. Dark blue clouds were building in the east. "Looks that way."

Eric swung down the ramp to the dock. His face was serious. "Listen, I must ask you something."

"Sure."

He took off his sunglasses and clipped them to the collar of his polo shirt. "Mama Alice called on me this morning."

David's stomach dropped. "Oh, yeah, about that. . ."

"Why did you go there? I asked you to leave her alone."

"I'm sorry. It wasn't something we planned. We just happened to take another trail down from La Tour. We ended up on the beach close to her house."

"But why did you tell her I sent you there?"

"That was my fault, I'm afraid," said a voice in David's ear. He turned to see Amy standing there.

"Why would you say such a thing?" Eric asked.

"I apologize," Amy said, stepping forward. "Sarah and I wanted to see the ceremony, and it seemed like a good idea to mention your name."

"Well, it wasn't. Mama Alice was not pleased with me."

"I'm sorry," Amy said. "I know it was wrong. And please don't be angry with David. It was me, not him."

Eric looked from her to David, then back to Amy.

"Did you see a ceremony?"

"Yes, we did," Amy said, nodding. "It was very interesting."

Eric unhooked the sunglasses from his shirt and placed them back on his face. "Those people are very protective of their beliefs and rituals," he said. "I hope no one besides Mama Alice knew you were there."

Amy's eyes narrowed. "You know, you lied to us, Eric. You said that YouTube video wasn't filmed here on St. Celine. But it was. The ritual in the video took place at the pavilion where we were the other night. I recognized everything."

Eric looked away, out toward the harbor. "Yes. It was filmed here."

"But I don't get it. Why lie to us?"

Eric whirled toward her. "To keep you away from things you do not understand." He stepped closer and lowered his voice. "Some of those people are dangerous," he said. "Believe me, girl, you do not want to get mixed up with them."

Amy looked at David, and he knew what she was thinking. "You know something, don't you?" she said to Eric. "You know something about Josh and Emily White."

Eric shook his head. "I know nothing."

"I don't believe you," she went on. "I think you know what happened to them."

Eric held up his hands. "Please. I can't say anything more."

David placed a hand on Amy's shoulder. "Just drop it."

She shot him a cold look, then brushed past him and up onto the *New Beginning*.

Eric looked at him, but his eyes were hidden by the

dark glasses. "I'm sorry, Todger."

David shook his head. "Don't worry about it."

The next hour was spent in uncomfortable silence as they secured their lines to the pilings, and when they were done, Eric headed back to his boat. He turned as he reached the top of the gangplank. "Listen," he said. "You get in trouble, you call me. Understand?"

David nodded. "Yes. Thank you."

"It's what friends do." And then he was out of sight.

David found Amy brooding on the sundeck. "Want some company?"

She turned to look at him and her face softened. "Sorry about that. I didn't mean to go all-out bitch back there."

He sat down beside her. "I'm sure if he knew anything he would have told the police. Eric's a good guy."

"I'm sure he is." She leaned back on her elbows, face up to the sky. "It's just that I thought Sarah was getting obsessive over the Whites, that she was seeing connections that just weren't there. Until we verified the video was made here on the island. Now I don't know." She looked at him. "I think there's more to the story. I think something's being covered up, and Eric knows more than he's letting on."

"You don't know that, Amy."

"No, I don't. But the fact that he lied to us is suspicious, don't you think?"

He couldn't argue with her there. He'd never known Eric to lie or to be involved in anything shady. And he couldn't imagine he would be involved in any way with the Whites' disappearance. "You know, Eric grew up here. His whole life is here. He knows these people a helluva lot better than I do. I'm sure he meant what he said, that he was trying to protect you and Sarah."

"I guess."

"So where is Sarah?"

"Shopping." Amy sat up. "She was sleepwalking again last night. I had to get her back in bed. And David. . ."

"Yes?"

"There was someone down in the courtyard watching us up on the balcony."

He looked at her. "What?"

"I'm sure of it. It's the second time we've seen him."

"Did you tell the front desk?"

"First thing this morning. They told me it was probably one of the staff on routine rounds."

"Well, that makes sense."

"That's what I thought, too. The first time. But last night was different. I could see his eyes, David. He definitely was watching us."

"What did he look like?"

"I couldn't tell. It was too dark."

He reached an arm around her. "Well, he certainly has good taste."

She frowned. "It was creepy. I almost called you."

"I would have been right there."

She leaned up and kissed his cheek. "I know. That's why I didn't bother you. I was just freaking out."

He stretched and lay back on the lounge. "I've done all I can do here on the boat for now."

She lay down beside him. "So now what? You just let it ride out the storm?"

"Yep. That's what we did during Sandy. This will be nothing compared to that."

She rolled over and laid her head on his shoulder, idly stroking his chest with her fingertips. "What are we gonna do?"

He pressed his face into her hair, inhaling the scent of honey and citrus, and closed his eyes. It was the question he had been asking himself all week. "You're gonna go back home on Sunday and I'm going back to work."

She sniffed and he realized she had started to cry. "I guess there's nothing else we can do, is there?"

He looked down at her. "Look, just because you go back home doesn't mean it's over. We've got email. Skype. The phone. You can come visit anytime. And who knows, maybe I'll take a little trip up to the States."

"I know."

"We just need to enjoy the rest of this week and not think about it."

"That's so hard to do."

He kissed her forehead. "I know it is." Something in his gut was boiling. He knew long-distance relationships rarely worked out. He knew that after Sunday they would probably never see each other again. And he had no idea how he would get through letting her go.

9

The street seemed oddly deserted this morning until Sarah realized many tourists were staying away because of the impending storm. She watched the ferry dock in the harbor, but its incoming load was light, dwarfed by the number of tourists waiting to leave the island. From the looks of the lobby of the inn this morning, a lot of people were checking out early and heading out before the weather got too bad. She wondered about her and Amy's decision to stay on through the storm, but according to the weather reports she had heard, there was not much to worry about. David didn't seem too concerned, and that comforted both of them.

She had awakened this morning with a screaming, nauseating headache and the awful realization of the things she had said to Amy. She had always remembered everything she did and said the few times she had been drunk, and this was one time she wished she could forget. She apologized again as the horrible words she had said rushed through her head with sickening clarity. Amy – bless her – told her to forget it, and Sarah could tell she meant it. Amy was going down to meet David at the marina, and Sarah refused to intrude; instead she decided to head down the hill to Ben Harbour. She couldn't help but wonder how Amy would take leaving David behind. She had never seen Amy so head-over-heels about a guy before, even the guys she'd dated for months. She had to admit, there was something about David that was charming, something she hadn't seen at first. But of course no man could ever compare to Robert.

She'd taken the early shuttle from the inn, and she'd had it all to herself. Marko was again the driver, and he seemed strangely distant, even though she greeted him warmly in spite of her slight hangover. She remembered how aloof he had been during their previous encounter with him their first day on the island and shrugged it off. It was too early to ruminate on imagined slights.

In town she headed for the Island Perk coffee shop and ordered a large latte. She sat at a tiny table in the front window, watching the other tourists and sipping her drink. It was rich and delicious and better than anything she'd ever had at Starbucks, and she figured it had at least twice as many calories as what she usually got there. But she was on vacation. Calories didn't count on vacation.

Feeling a little better after her caffeine fix, she strolled down the walk, glancing in at the shops as she passed. She still hadn't purchased a souvenir for herself. She didn't want anything else to set on a shelf to gather dust; she had plenty of those things – cheap and usually made in China. Still, she wanted something beautiful, something that would evoke memories of the island every time she looked at it. Maybe jewelry. Diamonds in the Bahamas were notoriously cheap, and even if she couldn't be sure of the quality, at the prices she had seen it didn't matter. After all, she wasn't looking for anything to wear to a black tie event.

On a whim she entered the next door along the way, a bright little shop that smelled of cinnamon and caramel and sold jewelry and trinkets. The dark-skinned girl at the counter looked up from her paperback and gave her a wide smile. Her black hair was covered in a pink kerchief. "Mirabel" was written crudely on her nametag with a black Sharpie. "Good morning, miss."

"Hi," Sarah said. She looked about the place, noticing the lack of other customers. "Not much going on in town today, huh?"

Mirabel shook her head. "Everyone getting ready for the storm. Not many people coming over from Nassau or the other islands."

"Any idea what time it's supposed to hit?"

"Radio say sometime this afternoon. You staying here on St. Celine?"

Sarah nodded. "St. Celine Inn. All week."

"You probably want to get back there right after lunchtime."

Sarah browsed through the racks of items. There were shell necklaces and leather bracelets, rings with gaudy costume-jewelry stones and stickpins embellished with curious designs.

"You looking for something in particular?" the girl asked.

Sarah ran her fingertips through a display of brightly-colored silk scarves. "Actually, yes. I want something special to remember my time here on the island. Something of quality."

Mirabel nodded. "I think I know what you want." She motioned Sarah toward the counter, toward the glass-covered case next to the cash register. "These are our best items here."

The case contained exquisite creations of diamonds and other gems in gold and silver settings, and they all looked prohibitively expensive. Mirabel brought out a pair of roundcut diamond leverback earrings. "These would look lovely on you," she said.

Sarah considered them for a moment. "They're nice, but not really what I had in mind."

The girl placed them gently back into the velvet stand. "Perhaps you are looking for something more authentic. Something that symbolizes the islands."

"Yes, exactly," Sarah said. "I want something unique, something I can't get back home."

Mirabel nodded. From beneath the display case she pulled out a long box and set it before Sarah. "You may find this to your liking." She opened the lid and Sarah gasped.

It was a braided rope chain holding a gold round pendant. At first Sarah thought it was a pumpkin – a jack o'lantern – but she quickly realized it was a skull wearing a pirate hat. The hat was encrusted with small rubies and chocolate diamonds, and the skull's teeth were gleaming white sapphires. Just below the mouth dangled a set of gold crossbones. It was beautiful, and nothing like she had ever seen before. "It's lovely," she said.

Mirabel held it up so Sarah could see the stones closer. "Is this more what you had in mind?"

Sarah found herself nodding. "It's *exactly* what I

had in mind." She reached out a fingertip to the cross-bones.

"The skull is eighteen-karat gold and the gems are highest quality."

Sarah withdrew her hand. "I'm terrified to ask how much this is."

Mirabel laughed. "Shopping here is duty-free, so it is not near as much as you probably think." She turned the box over and pointed to the tag. Five hundred dollars.

Sarah blew out a breath. "That's still a little more than I wanted to spend."

The girl cocked her head. "For you, I make it four hundred."

Sarah chewed her lip. The pendant really was what she had been looking for. And it would most likely be the only thing she bought for herself this week. Still, she thought she should negotiate a bit more. "How about three-fifty?"

Mirabel nodded. "T'ree fifty it is, miss."

Sarah took a deep breath. "You do take Visa, right?"

10

Mirabel watched the fair-skinned woman leave the shop, proudly wearing the skull and crossbones pendant.

She recognized her as soon as she had come through the door. Remembered her stumbling up to the temple crying and confused, beseeching Mama Alice for forgiveness for violating the sacred ceremony. Of course she did not know they had drawn her there with Mama Alice's ritual, pulled her in as easily as reeling in a fish. Bacalou had been hungry for a mate; it had been two years since he had satisfied himself with a woman of fair skin. But they had all learned from the Bad Business then. This time there would be no mistakes. Mama Alice had made sure of that.

It had been so easy to steer the woman toward the symbol of Bacalou. His countenance was imprinted in her mind as deeply as that of her own mother. She would respond to the mark even if she didn't understand why. And now that she possessed the pendant it would be even easier to bring her into the temple for Bacalou's bidding. The woman was ripe, and Bacalou needed an heir.

Mirabel smiled. Mama Alice would be proud.

II

The first rain began to fall at 3:30.

David persuaded Amy to go back to the inn, sending her off from the marina with a kiss she tasted all the way back through town. "We'll talk tomorrow," he said.

"You promise?"

"Of course I do. You go be with Sarah now."

She nuzzled into his chest. "I'd rather go be with you."

"Tomorrow." He looked down at her. "We'll plant Sarah at the hotel bar and spend the whole day in bed."

A thrill shot through her. Spending the day making love while the storm clashed outside sounded like heaven. "Why can't we start now and keep going all night?"

He kissed her forehead. "'Cause I got stuff to do at the house. And Sarah needs you."

She took a deep breath. Yes, Sarah certainly did need her. After last night Amy was afraid to let her sleep alone in the room. She wondered what would happen when they returned to Cedar Hill. If she got worse, who would watch over her then? She leaned up and kissed him on the lips. "I expect you to be in the hotel lobby by ten in the morning."

"I'll be there."

She started toward the golf cart, looking back over her shoulder. "Even it's coming a monsoon."

He smiled at her. "Even if I have to swim."

The first drops of rain pelted the roof of the cart as she drove away, but she barely noticed. It was only after she passed the edge of town and started the climb up the hill to the inn that she realized she had a smile plastered on her face. And it had David written all over it.

Sarah was watching TV when she reached the room. A weather report from the station in Nassau. "The worst part won't hit until after midnight," she said. "Only light rain until then."

"I guess we just sit tight," Amy said, sinking onto the bed beside her.

"It's still technically a depression," Sarah said. "Not even a tropical storm."

"That's bad enough," Amy said. "Are they still saying it will be out of here by tomorrow?"

"Yep," Sarah said. "Everything should clear up by the afternoon."

Amy looked at her. "You seem awfully chipper."

"Yeah, I had a fun day."

Amy nodded and smiled at her. "Good. I'm glad."

"Oh," Sarah said, "look at this. It's what I bought myself today." She held out pendant that was strung around her neck.

Amy stared at it. It was a hideous skull and crossbones covered with gemstones. "Wow," she said.

Sarah was grinning. "What do you think? Isn't it great? I found it in one of the shops downtown and I just had to get it. I've never seen anything like it."

"It's certainly unique," Amy said. Truthfully, she had no idea what to say. It was the ugliest thing she had ever seen. But Sarah seemed so proud of it that Amy could never say so. "Can I ask how much you paid for it?"

"Three fifty."

"Three *hundred* and fifty?" Jesus Christ.

"I know I probably paid too much," Sarah gushed, "but I *love* it."

There was something wild and manic in Sarah's eyes, a giddiness. Something unnerving. "Are you taking your medication?" Amy asked her.

Sarah sighed. "Yes, Mother. Every morning, just like I'm supposed to."

Amy looked at her. "Have you had any more. . . episodes?"

Sarah's eyes narrowed. "What?"

"You know," Amy said, "hallucinations. Visions of Robert."

"Oh, that," Sarah said with a smile. "I'm chalking that up to exhaustion. And no, I haven't seen any more 'ghosts.'" She reached out and took Amy's hand. "I can't thank you enough for talking me into coming here. This has been really good for me."

The rain continued to fall outside, tapping on the balcony and the window panes, punctuated by lightning and crashes of thunder. Amy flipped channels until she found a documentary on Caribbean pirates, and they watched it while dozing on and off until their stomachs told them it was time for dinner.

Downstairs, the hotel restaurant was nearly deserted, and their waiter, Edward, seemed genuinely delighted to have someone to serve. "Tonight you get extra-special attention," he told them as he took their order.

When he left Amy whispered, "'Cause he wants an extra-special tip," and Sarah giggled.

The power went out just as Edward was setting down their main courses, leaving the dining room in a gray half-light. Through the windows overlooking the gardens they watched the palms and shrubs dance in the wind. Raindrops splattered against the glass, turning the panes into a waterfall. Edward returned with a lit candle for their table, all smiles and good humor. "Now we make it nice and romantic. It's a shame you do not have two nice fellows to share it with."

"Any idea how long the power will be out?" Sarah asked.

"The inn has a generator," Edward said, "but sometimes it does not want to cooperate." At that moment, the lights blazed on, then dimmed to an unsteady flicker. "There we are," he said. "I leave the candle here just in case."

They ate their meal in the dim light of the flickering chandeliers. Lightning flashed and thunder boomed, and Amy couldn't help but feel they were dining in the Haunted Mansion at Disneyland. "This is kind of creepy," she said.

Sarah laughed. "Think of it as an adventure. Something we can tell everyone when we get back." She cut a slice of her chicken breast. "Of course, you'll have a holiday fling to talk about."

"Yeah," Amy said, feeling her stomach knot up. "Look, I know I haven't been a very good companion on this trip. I know I've just left you hanging a couple of times."

Sarah shook her head. "No, it's all right." She wiped her mouth on her napkin. "I know I apologized already for saying all those things, but I really am sorry I blurted all that out."

"Well, they probably needed to be said."

"It really hasn't been as bad as I made it out to be. It's been fun. Really."

Amy folded her napkin and placed it beside her plate. She suddenly wasn't very hungry. "Sarah, what am I going to do? Every time I think about Sunday I just want to curl up in a ball and cry my eyes out."

"What does David say about it?"

"He keeps mentioning email and Skype and me coming down here to visit. Sarah, we both know that won't work. I have enough trouble trying to keep a man when he lives in the same town."

"But maybe this is different. You said yourself you've never met anyone else like him. It could happen this time."

"You really think so?"

"It just depends on how bad you want it to work out."

At that moment, Amy caught a glimpse of the old Sarah, the one before the accident, the one she'd confided in and grown close to. It was like meeting up with an old friend. She reached out and took Sarah's hand. "I'm sorry I've caused all this drama. This wasn't supposed to be about me. This whole trip was to get you out of your funk. To show you life is still worth living, even after all you went through."

"And it has," Sarah said. "Really."

Amy took a sip of her wine. "So how do you think you'll handle things when you get back home?"

Sarah nodded. "Good. I've really cleared my head this week. It's not that I don't still love Robert – *miss* him – but I'm letting go of the pain. These past few days have helped me do that." She dropped her gaze. "I'm thinking about putting the house up for sale when I get back."

Amy looked at her. "Are you serious?"

"I don't need all that room. Why do I want a four-bedroom house?"

"But it was your dream house."

"Mine and *Robert's* dream house. It's way too big for one person. We'd planned to make a life together there, raise a family. For just me it would be a burden. All that maintenance on an old house. All the yard work." She smiled. "But it would be perfect for you and David."

Amy shook her head. "I don't even want to go there."

"But you'll have to live somewhere. And think about all that room for his record collection."

"I'm not buying your house, Sarah." She blew out a breath. "Besides, I'm sure we'll need someplace with a bigger garage to store a boat."

☠.☃.☠

Upstairs, the TV was showing nothing but snow, and although the rain had let up, darkness had descended abruptly leaving a black emptiness outside the windows highlighted only by occasional flashes of lightning.

Sarah lay down on her bed and looked at her phone. "Wi-fi's still working."

Amy sat next to her. "Can you pull up a weather report?"

"Let's see. . ." Sarah poked around on her screen until she managed to pull up a radar image. The main storm was moving closer but was still two hundred miles out. "Looks like the worst might hit around three in the morning. Sustained winds at twenty-five miles an hour. Hasn't strengthened any."

Amy stretched out on her own bed. "That's good." This sucked. No television, no place to go with the rain pounding outside. She'd brought along an old Stephen King novel, but she didn't think she could bear to try to read with the flickering lights.

She wondered what David was doing. If he had power, he was probably listening to old records. If not, he was most likely sitting on the sofa watching the storm and drinking beer. She physically ached to touch him, to be cuddled against him while the rain pounded on the roof and the thunder shook the walls. She picked up her phone. If it wasn't so damned expensive to use it down here she would give him a call. Just to talk. Just to hear his voice.

Instead, she found herself scrolling through her pictures. Snapshots of the island from David's boat. The view of the town from the trail up to La Tour. David sitting in the pool below the waterfall, smiling at the camera and leaned back against a wall of rock, his hand in his wet hair. She felt her eyes begin to water. She had to stop this. She was starting to obsess, and that was never a good thing.

She placed the phone on the nightstand and rolled over onto her side away from Sarah, bearing down against the hollow, sick feeling in her stomach. She was not going to let herself cry, not now, not with Sarah in the room continuing to chatter on about the coming storm. This wasn't supposed to happen. She wasn't supposed to fall in love with him. She wasn't even supposed to sleep with him. She stared at the wall and willed the tears to dry.

"I'm putting my flashlight on the nightstand," Sarah said.

"Flashlight?"

"I always pack one. You never know. We might need it to get to the bathroom if the power goes out again."

"Okay." Whatever. If she would only stop talking.

"I think I'm going to read for a while."

Thank God. "Okay."

"You all right?"

"Just tired. What'cha reading?" She knew Sarah had a Kindle app on her phone and was always downloading free and cheap books.

"It's about ghost hunters in a haunted movie theater."

"You sure you should be reading that kind of stuff?" The last thing she needed was Sarah sleepwalking *and* having nightmares.

"I'll be all right."

Amy grunted and closed her eyes. She could sure use a cup of tea. Or a beer. Something, anything to do to get her mind off David.

She sighed and rolled over to grab her book. She might as well try to read, too. But after a few pages she found herself nodding off, reading paragraphs over because they weren't making sense. She finally put the book down and decided to get ready for bed. It was only a little after eight, but she was exhausted.

After brushing her teeth, she climbed under the covers and stared at the ceiling. Sarah had turned out the lamp, but the glow from her phone and the thunder kept Amy from drifting on into sleep. Not to mention she was thinking about David again and how she looked forward to seeing him in the morning. After a while she put the other pillow over her head and closed her eyes, trying to concentrate on the rhythm of her breathing. She wondered if Sarah would give her one of her pills to help her sleep, but decided she'd better not ask about that. Finally, she felt herself drifting off, slipping out of consciousness into the place where thoughts were disjointed and fleeting.

She was back at La Tour. But not just her. All three of them. She and David were standing in the pool at the base of the waterfall. They were looking up to the top of the cliff where the water was plummeting over. Sarah was there, standing at the very edge of the outcropping of rock, her toes hanging over into nothingness. She was smiling. Amy and David were motioning her to go back, to come down to safety. Sarah was naked except for the skull and crossbones pendant. Its mouth was moving, and Amy could see that it was trying to grab hold of Sarah's flesh. Sarah moved, and the pendant swung and its hideous mouth grabbed hold of her breast, tearing into the skin with razor-sharp teeth. Blood ran down Sarah's stomach as the thing continued to chew. Bits of flesh were flying as the pendant, now a living yet undead thing, gnawed its way to the bone. Sarah continued to smile, even as droplets of blood flecked her face from the skull's incessant chewing. Amy reached for David. But he was gone. Instead the masked, shirtless man from the video stood there, his muscular chest splashed with white paint and blood. He grabbed for her. She screamed.

Amy sat up in the bed. The power was off again and thunder was crashing outside. She reached for her phone and checked the time: 1:20. A sudden flash of lightning illuminated the room. Sarah's bed was empty.

Her phone lay among the rumpled sheets, its screen black. "Sarah, where are you?" She was answered only by a rumble of thunder.

She felt around on the nightstand and felt the flashlight. She grabbed it and flicked it on, shining it about the room. "Sarah?"

She slipped out of bed and checked the bathroom. Nothing. Where was she?

Amy froze. The door to the hallway was standing wide open. The light disappeared into the blackness beyond. She peered out, shining the light up and down the hall. "Sarah?" she whispered. Shit. This was ridiculous.

Back in the room she quickly stepped into her clothes and grabbed her phone. To hell with the cost, she was calling David. She couldn't deal with this by herself. She punched in his number and waited. Nothing connected. She checked her screen. There was no signal. The cell tower must be offline.

She stepped into the hallway and headed toward the stairs. Above the sound of the rain and thunder, she could hear a buzz of conversation from down below. In the dimly-lit lobby several guests milled about, talking loudly about the storm and guzzling drinks from the bar. A man and a woman were on duty behind the front desk, their faces illuminated by candles. Thank God. "Excuse me," she said to them.

"Yes, miss?" the woman said.

"I can't find my friend. Did you see anyone come through here?"

"Several people," the man said. "We have had many down here asking about the power. I'm afraid our generator – "

"She sleepwalks and she's not in the room. Her

name's Sarah Dunham. She's fairly tall, longish blonde hair." She tried to remember what Sarah was wearing. "She might have been wearing a large gold pendant."

The woman looked up. "A skull and crossbones?"

"Yes!" Thank God.

The man and woman exchanged a glance. "I saw her talking with Marko, one of our shuttle drivers," the woman said.

Amy let out a breath of relief. "Oh, good." So she wasn't sleepwalking.

The woman looked at her curiously. "I noticed the pendant because it was the symbol for Bacalou. Very unusual for someone like her to be wearing."

Amy stared at her. "Did you say Bacalou?"

"Yes. Bacalou is – "

Amy held up her hand. "I know who he is. Did you see where she went afterwards? Maybe toward the bar?"

The man moved closer. "She and Marko went out the front doors."

Oh, shit. "Do you think he drove her to town?"

The woman shook her head. "Our shuttle doesn't run this late."

"Anyplace else they could have gone?"

"They may be out on the portico," the man said. "I did not see them come back in." He smiled. "Perhaps your friend has taken a fancy to our Marko."

Amy left the desk and headed out the front doors and was immediately hit with wind-driven rain. She shined the flashlight around. "Sarah!" No one was here, and if they were, they would have been soaked.

She stiffened. The hotel shuttle was gone from its spot in the covered drive just off the portico. So they had taken the van after all. And there was only one place they could have gone. The pavilion in the forest.

Back in the lobby, the man at the front desk looked up from his work. "Did you find your friend?"

"No," she said. If she could just get to David's, he would know what to do. "The shuttle's gone. Can I get a cab or something here?"

"I'm sorry, miss, but there are no cabs on the island. Even if there were, I'm afraid the phone lines are down at the moment."

Fuck. She would have to take the golf cart.

The woman looked at her. "Did you say the shuttle was gone?"

"Yes. I didn't think it ran after midnight."

She smiled. "Marko must have taken a keen interest in your friend to take her out after hours. And in this weather."

Amy left them and headed upstairs to get the key to the cart. It would not be a comfortable ride, but at least it had a roof and headlights. She only hoped the windshield wiper worked.

In the room she grabbed the key from the nightstand. She almost grabbed her hoodie, but then decided it would be useless against the rain. It certainly wasn't cold outside, and struggling in a wet fleece jacket would be more uncomfortable than damp clothes.

Back outside, she started up the cart and found the light switch. The panel blazed on. After a moment of searching, she found the control for the wiper. It moved agonizingly slow, but it was better than nothing. She backed out of the space and headed down the hill toward town. Her shorts and t-shirt were already soaked through before she was out of the parking lot.

The main drag was deserted, and the darkened shops made the street look like a ghost town. As she suspected, there was no sign here of the shuttle. Toward the marina she could see nothing but blackness, and she fleetingly wondered how David's boat was weathering the storm.

As she came to the end of the street, she slowed to a crawl. The pavement ended here, and she thought about the horrible road that led to David's and the pavilion beyond. What would it be like in this mess?

She checked her phone again, hoping by some miracle she would have a signal and she could call David to come meet her in town. But there was nothing. She would have to chance it.

She pulled off the paved street and headed up the gravel lane. It wasn't as bad as she had feared, though rivulets of rainwater flowed across the road in places. The wheels hit a large hole with a splash, and she nearly slipped out of the seat. She clung to the wheel and managed to steer the cart back on course.

She could barely see the road in the dim headlights through the driving rain and the smeared windshield. Just a mile through this until she reached David's house. Just a mile. She pulled the wet hair from her eyes and squinted into the nothingness ahead of her. It was as if she were heading into a black hole. What if she misjudged the distance from the main street? What if in the darkness she completely missed David's house and kept going past it?

The cart hit a rut with a thud, slamming the steering wheel into her chest. She tried turning, but the wheel wouldn't budge. The tires spun and she could feel the cart slipping backwards down the hill. She shifted into reverse and felt the gears engage, then inched back a few feet and put the cart into drive. The tiny motor groaned as the wheels sought purchase. She wasn't moving. She reversed the engine again. This time the cart stayed put. Back into drive. The tires spun with a whine.

She turned off the motor and dug the flashlight out of her pocket, then shined it down the side of the cart. The wheels were up to their axles in mud. Fuck.

She stepped out into the downpour and her feet went ankle-deep into the cold water rushing through the rut. The cart was stuck. She would have to walk the rest of the way.

She pointed her flashlight ahead into the blackness and set off.

12

At first, David thought it was the thunder that had awakened him. He was coming out of a dream where he and Amy were standing at the bottom of La Tour. Sarah was at the top of the cliff. Something was eating her. Chewing on her. She was naked and bleeding and laughing.

He opened his eyes and heard the noise again. Someone was pounding on the front door. He whipped off the covers and felt around for his shorts. "Coming!" Damn, it was black as pitch. The power must be out. He grabbed the flashlight from his nightstand drawer and stepped into the hall, nearly tripping over Seymour, who took off through the house with a startled cry.

He made his way through the kitchen into the living room. "Who's there?"

"It's Amy!"

He pulled open the door and she spilled into the room, landing in his arms. "What the hell are you doing out in this?" he said. He looked behind her at the blackness outside. "Did you walk?"

"Fucking golf cart is stuck in the mud about half a mile back." She was soaked through and her hair was plastered to her head.

"Come in, we've got to get you out of those wet clothes. What're you doing here?"

"Sarah's gone again!"

"What?"

She followed him through the house to the bathroom, telling him about waking up to find Sarah's bed empty and the clerks at the front desk seeing her leave with Marko. She pulled off her shirt and laid it over the edge of the tub. "I think they've gone back to the temple."

David pulled a couple of towels from the shelf. "Why do you think that?" He stepped into the bedroom to pull a pair of shorts and a t-shirt for Amy from the dresser. "They could have gone anywhere."

"It's the only thing that makes any sense." She draped her bra beside the t-shirt and stepped out of her shorts. "She got this pendant in town today. She was wearing it when she left. One of the desk clerks said it was the symbol for Bacalou."

He aimed the flashlight at the ceiling, filling the room with muted light. "Wait, is that one of those spirits or whatever?"

She squeezed one of the towels around her hair. "Yes. The bad one. The one we saw depicted in the video." She threw down the towel and took the clothes from David. "The other night when I caught her sleepwalking, she kept saying that name over and over. 'Bacalou.' And I could hear those drums in the distance, like there was another ceremony going on. I'm terrified. If she went back to the temple with Marko, there's no telling what they're doing to her."

"I think you're overreacting."

"Am I?" She wriggled into the shirt – a souvenir from an old 5K in Indy. "You saw the video. And you heard what Eric said. It's real, David. We've got to get out to that place and check on her."

"In this storm?"

She stepped into the shorts and pulled the drawstring tight. "I'm really worried. We've got to go see."

"And if she's not there?"

"We go to the police. She's on this island some-where."

David felt a chill pass through him. "You're right." He leaned forward and kissed her. "Let me get dressed. We'll take my bike."

☠☀☠

Moments later, with Amy wrapped in a poncho be-hind him, they were heading up the road through the downpour on the Honda. He had no idea how Amy had made it as far in the golf cart as she did. Even with his headlight on bright it was impossible to see more than a few feet before them. It was only by chance he hap-pened to spot the dirt lane veering off to the right.

If there was a gathering at the pavilion, David won-dered if they would even hear them coming above the storm and the drums. From what he could recall, the pavilion had a metal roof, and this rain pounding on top of it had to be deafening. It might be possible to get close enough to see without anyone knowing.

Suddenly through the trees he saw the flickering glow from the temple. There were tiki torches en-sconced along the walls and support beams, and he could see people swaying and moving about and hear the drums above the rain. He doused the headlight.

"There's the hotel shuttle," Amy said, pointing to a white van among several other vehicles. "They're here."

David killed the engine and coasted to a stop. "Follow me," he said, leading her toward the back of the van. Carefully they peeked around at the activity in the pavilion.

"Oh, my God," Amy whispered.

Through the dancing, chanting congregation they could see Sarah. She was naked and strapped to a table. Her legs were spread wide and dangled over the edge. Between them was the muscular, dark-skinned man from the video, his torso slathered with white. He, too, was naked except for a wooden mask covering his face, a mask painted with a red skull. He was working his hips rhythmically with the beat of the drums, steadily and furiously. Sarah was laughing and writhing on the table, seemingly in ecstasy. The pendant lolled between her breasts, gleaming in the torchlight. Suddenly the man between her legs stiffened. The drums reached a frenzied beat, then stopped as the man in the mask relaxed and moved away from Sarah.

The congregation was quiet and still. No one had noticed David and Amy enter the pavilion. Amy stepped forward, away from David before he could grab her. "What the fuck's going on here?"

They all turned toward them, shining black faces and wide eyes in the flickering light. The naked man in the mask still stood between Sarah's legs, his erection wilted and spent. No one moved.

Sarah giggled on the table, moving as much as her restraints would allow. "Amy? Amy is that you?"

Amy rushed to Sarah's side pulling at the knots on

the ropes. "Yes, baby, it's me. We'll get you out of here.

"Isn't it wonderful?" Sarah said, her lips curled into a satisfied smile. "I'm going to have Bacalou's baby."

Amy glanced around at the frozen congregation. "What have you done to her?" She pulled on the ropes and looked at David. "Help me!"

David took a step toward the table. His keychain had a small knife on it. He reached for his pocket.

Suddenly, Amy's eyes went wide. "Look out!"

Intense, blinding pain reverberated through his skull, and he felt himself falling. He seemed to fall forever. And then everything went black.

☠☠☠

The first thing he was aware of was that the back of his head hurt like fuck. He was sitting on the ground, leaning back against something hard and rocky. He reached a hand to his head and felt his hair matted with dried blood.

"David!"

He opened his eyes. Everything was blurry, but he could make out that he was in a cave. There was one flickering torch attached to the wall throwing off ghostly shadows on the craggy walls. He turned and saw Amy beside him. "What happened?"

"Are you all right? One of those guys clubbed you over the head with a liquor bottle and knocked you out."

He shook his head. "I think I'm okay. How long was I out?"

"Couple of hours."

"Sarah?"

"I'm over here," came a soft voice.

He could see her, dressed now but barefoot, curled

into a ball on the other side of him. He moved to stand and reach for her, but something caught his ankle. He looked down. An iron shackle, its chain bolted to the cave wall. "What the fuck? Where are we?"

"A cave behind Mama Alice's house," Amy said. "They brought us here right after they attacked you. They took our phones, our keys, everything."

"Amy, I'm so sorry," Sarah said. She was sobbing, her hands covering her head. "I never meant for this to happen. I never meant to get us all in trouble."

"It's okay, baby," Amy said.

"I don't know how I even got back here with Marko. All I remember is being on that table and seeing you and David coming through the crowd."

"It's all right," Amy said. "They did something to you. It's not your fault."

"Wait," David said, "*who* brought us here?"

"A bunch of them," Amy said. "They brought us in here and chained us up. The storm's worse. The rain. I think it may flood in here."

Panic seized his belly. "We've got to get out of here." He looked at the shackle again. It looked old and rusted, held together a bolt and a nut. Still solid. He pulled on it, but there was no give. The nut was stuck tight; it wasn't going to move.

"Ah, my friends," said a voice. A dark-skinned man stood at the front of the cave. He wore a pair of white shorts and a blue polo shirt, and the white paint that had adorned his arms had mostly been washed away in the rain. "I see you are awake, Mr. David."

David glared at him. "Who are you?"

The man smiled broadly. "I go by many names," he said. "In this place I am known as Marko. A simple shuttle driver for the inn. But I am first and foremost a servant to Bacalou."

"Where are we?"

Marko motioned about the room. "This cave is a remnant of St. Celine's slavery days. Mama Alice's house once belonged to a slave trader. This was where the merchandise was stored while waiting for the ships to take it to its final destination."

"Merchandise," Amy said. "You mean slaves."

Marko shrugged. "Of course."

She looked at him. "What do you want from us?"

Marko laughed. "Well, of course now that you have seen we cannot let you go. It's something we will have to. . . take care of."

"You're going to kill us, aren't you?" David said. "You're going to leave us here to drown when the storm surge hits, aren't you?"

"What a great idea," Marko said. "But no. The water will not get up this high." He smiled. "Mama Alice has something special planned for you two."

"Us two?" Amy said. "What about Sarah?"

Marko kneeled and reached out a hand to Sarah's tear-streaked face. "We certainly cannot harm Miss Sarah," he said. "She is the one who has been chosen. Chosen to bear the seed of Bacalou."

"You bastard," Amy said. "Is this what you did to Josh and Emily White?"

Marko stood and stepped toward her. "Miss Emily was barren. But we found her to be useful in other ways. Mr. Josh. . . now he is another story."

Amy glared at him. "What did you do to them, you bunch of sick fucks? You raped Emily, just like you did Sarah, didn't you? Then what? Carved them up for one of your rituals? Dumped their bodies out at sea so they'd never be found?"

"Sarah was right all along," David said. "They never left the island, did they?"

"You helped cover it up, didn't you?" Amy said to Marko. "You work for the inn. You got rid of their stuff, didn't you? Cleaned out their room, made it look like they up and left."

Marko smiled at her coldly. "By morning, the two girls sharing Room 204 will have also left. Suddenly gone in the night, taking all their belongings. But a certain shuttle driver will remember driving them to the pier to catch a ferry to one of the neighboring islands to spend their last few days of holiday; which one, he cannot recall. He sees so many guests and hears so many things."

"You know we'll be missed," David said. "I know people on this island. They'll come looking for me."

"You know," Marko said, "it is a funny thing. I recall seeing Mr. David Burke departing with the ladies. Maybe they were going on a trip together. Maybe they all three run away. You have become chummy the past few days, right?" He reached out and pinched Amy's cheek. "Especially with this one, no?"

David lunged at Marko but the shackle caught his ankle and brought him down to the hard floor of the cave. "You son-of-a-bitch."

Marko laughed. "You might as well relax, Mr. David. It will all be over soon."

13

Marko led Sarah through the downpour, across the muddy yard to Mama Alice's back porch and through the back screen door into the cluttered, candle-lit kitchen. The house was cold and smelled of vinegar and ashes.

Mama Alice stood at the counter with her back to them, busying herself with something in the sink. "Make sure she wipes her feet, Marko."

"She is pretty muddy," Marko said. "It's raining like a pissing cow."

"Do as best you can. We'll clean her up."

Marko grabbed Sarah's ankle and dragged her bare foot across the rough braided mat by the door, then did the same to the other one. He motioned to a cane bottom chair at the end of the kitchen table. "Sit."

"Marko," Mama Alice said from the sink, "go check to make sure everything is ready outside. And bring me a black rooster."

"Yes, Mama Alice." He pulled up the collar to his shirt and returned to the rain and the dark.

The chair creaked as Sarah sank into it. She looked at the hoard of items in front of her on the table. Mason jars holding desiccated leaves and unidentifiable objects, bottles filled with various powders and strangely colored liquids. She shivered, partly from the cold, and partly from the fact that some of the items suspended in the jars looked like creatures. And some looked. . . *alive*.

"You cold, child?" Mama Alice said without looking at her. She was barely audible above the drumming of the rain on the roof.

Sarah hugged herself and tried to stop her trembling. "I'm freezing. I got soaked in the rain."

"Would you like Mama Alice to make you some tea?"

Sarah glared at the back of Mama Alice's red-kerchief covered head. "No, I don't want any more of your fucking tea."

Mama Alice clucked her tongue and turned to look at Sarah over her shoulder. "Language, child. The vessel for Bacalou's offspring should behave better than that."

"I just want to get out of here," Sarah said. Her voice was trembling. Any moment now she would start crying again. "I want to get off this damned island and get back home." She held her shaking hands out to Mama Alice. "Please just let us go. We won't tell anyone anything. Just let us walk away from all this and we won't say a word."

Mama Alice reached out and took Sarah's hands. "Your fingers are like ice, child. We'll get you a blanket and get your feet cleaned up." She looked toward the doorway to the rest of the house and spoke something loudly in French.   All Sarah understood was *serviette*.

"Please, Mama Alice," Sarah said.   "We'll – *I'll* do anything.   Just don't hurt us."

"I have no intention of harming you, child."   She traced her fingers around the edge of Sarah's face, and Sarah caught a whiff of something putrid and dead. "You are the chosen one.   We have to take extra-special care of you."   She looked up.   "Oh, here are your things."

A warm blanket was laid across Sarah's shoulders, and she looked up to see a young, pale woman shuffling in with a dishpan and a towel.   She knelt at Sarah's feet and placed them in the warm soapy water.   "Thank you," Sarah whispered.

The girl looked up just as lightning flashed outside. Her eyes were the same milky white as the little girl from the ceremony.   And yet, Sarah recognized those eyes.   She knew them.   She had seen them over and over on the internet.   She reached out and touched the pallid face, brushed the dark hair from the forehead. "Emily," she said.   "Emily White?"

The girl tilted her head at Sarah, and the ghostly eyes blinked.

Sarah looked at Mama Alice.   "This is Emily White!"

"Yes, child," Mama Alice said.   She had returned to mixing something in a bowl.

Emily began methodically scrubbing Sarah's feet. "What's wrong with her?" Sarah said.   "What did you do to her?"

Mama Alice turned from the sink and looked at Emily with a hint of sadness.   "We thought Emily had been well-chosen. She was eager and beautiful, just like you. Unfortunately there was one thing we did not count on, and that was her inability to carry a child."

"So you what, turned her into a fucking *zombie*?"

"No, not zombie. A *jumbee* – one who is dead, yet awake because her body has been possessed by a spirit."

Tears stung Sarah's eyes. "But she can be cured, right?"

"There is no cure for *jumbee*. She will continue to live in this state until the flesh falls off her bones."

The chill in Sarah's body gave way to incomprehensible horror. "Does she. . . *feel*?"

"Physical pain and pleasure, yes. It's how I taught her to obey simple commands."

"But does she *know*? Does she know what's happened to her?"

Mama Alice looked at Emily curiously. "Hard to say. Sometimes when she is still she makes a sound almost like weeping. But she has no tears to cry."

Sarah stared at Mama Alice. "You're a monster! You've killed her. Now she's just a walking corpse."

"A corpse that can still be productive for the glory of Bacalou."

Sarah shook her head. "You're crazy! You're all fucking *insane*!" A sudden dread settled over her. "You're going to do this to me, aren't you? You're going to turn me into one of these *things*."

Mama Alice had cleared a space on one end of the wooden table. She covered it with a white cloth, mumbling a few words in what sounded like French, but Sarah wasn't sure.

"What did you do to Josh?" Sarah cried. "Is he one of these things, too?

"Not exactly," Mama Alice said, carefully placing bits of dried corn into a circle on the cloth.

Emily had finished washing Sarah's feet and was now patting them dry with a towel. "You killed him, though, didn't you? He's dead, isn't he?"

Mama Alice pulled two long slimy things from one of the jars. They appeared to be red peppers, but they were moving and making mewling sounds from tiny round mouths. "Oh, you'll see Mr. Josh soon enough," Mama Alice said. She gave an impatient glance at the back door. "Where is Marko with that rooster?"

Emily took the dirty pan of water and left the room, barely lifting her feet as she shambled through the doorway into the darkness of the hallway. Sarah watched her go, icy dread spreading through her. She had to get out of here. She had to make it back to town and find the police. But she had no idea which way the town was. And even if she did, how could she make it there in this storm?

The screen door creaked open and Marko carried in a small black rooster, swinging it by its feet. The cock clucked and flapped its wings, sending a few stray feathers floating through the kitchen. Mama Alice looked up from her preparations. "Ah, just in time. I am ready to begin."

She uncorked a bottle of white powder and began to sprinkle it on the cloth around the corn, using it to draw symbols and shapes, all the while chanting and singing. The words sounded strange – not French, not English – like no language Sarah had ever heard. Mama Alice reached for the two eyeless mewling creatures and dropped them into the center of the cloth on top of the grain. They shrieked and began to wither. Within seconds they were still and stiff. Mama Alice picked up a paring knife and chopped them into pieces, continuing her incomprehensible mutterings as she did so, then placed the pieces in her mouth and began to chew.

Sarah fought the urge to gag. She looked away, concentrating on the bare wooden floorboards.

Mama Alice took the rooster from Marko and held it above the items on the cloth, forcing its head down to the corn. The cock looked at them for a moment and began to peck. Mama Alice mumbled something and turned the rooster upside down, grabbing its legs and snapping them in two with a loud pop. The rooster fluttered and cackled.

This time Sarah couldn't hold back. She doubled over and vomited onto the floor.

Mama Alice didn't look at her. Instead, she grabbed one of the rooster's wings and broke it with a crack, then did the same with the other. The cock continued to writhe in her hands, but it was no longer making any sounds. With one swift movement, Mama Alice grabbed up a butcher knife and chopped the rooster's head from its body, spraying the white cloth and the table with blood. She had continued to chew all this time, and now she spat the contents of her mouth onto the cock's head, covering its sightless eyes with reddish goo. She handed the flopping rooster's body to Marko and raised her hands, her eyes closed, chanting louder now, almost singing. Suddenly she stopped.

Lightning flashed and the whole house shook with thunder.

Marko still held the bloody corpse of the rooster. "Is it finished?"

"Yes," Mama Alice whispered, her eyes still closed.

Before she could stop herself, Sarah leaped from the chair and burst through the screen door out into the rain.

From the kitchen behind her, Mama Alice called out, "You can't get away, child."

Sarah stood in the middle of the downpour, the sandy mud squishing between her bare toes. It was completely black out here. What would she do now? She needed a weapon, something to defend herself. Something to stop Marko and Mama Alice and give her time to free Amy and David.

A bolt of lightning cracked overhead, illuminating the chopping block in the side yard. The ax still stood embedded by the blade. She slogged toward it, stubbing her toe on a large stone. If she could get back to the cave, maybe they could use the ax to break the shackles. She grabbed the handle, prying it loose from the block.

She had just turned to head toward the cave when she heard a noise behind her. The inverted cross on the pile of rocks nearby was leaning, and several of the black stones were rolling away. The rain must have dislodged them.

Lightning flashed again, and this time she could see the stones moving, undulating, as if something was writhing beneath them. The cross fell away and slid down the pile of rocks.

No. Something wasn't right. This wasn't the rain doing this. It was something else. Sarah stood frozen, gripping the handle of the ax with her numb fingers.

Something emerged from the top of the rock pile. Something that moved. Something that looked like a hand. It felt about, seeking purchase, and then was followed by another. Two hands. Two arms. Reaching upward.

No. She could not be seeing this. It was just like

her hallucination of Robert in the attic. It wasn't real. She knew she was crazy this time.

A streak of lightning blazed across the sky, and she clearly saw the face as the arms continued to dig their way from the grave. The eyes were clouded marbles, the mouth open and slack beneath a scraggly black beard.

No! Oh, my God, no!

The white limbs pushed through the black stones, and the upper torso emerged. Beneath the thing's head, something glinted at its throat. It was a silver shark's tooth necklace. The one Josh White had been wearing.

Panic broke her paralysis, and she turned and fled toward the cave.

Marko emerged from the darkness in front of her. "Where you think you going, girl?"

She glanced over her shoulder. The Josh-thing was still crawling from the pile of rocks.

Marko followed her gaze. "Ah, I see Mama Alice's ritual was effective."

"Get out of my way," Sarah said.

"What you going to do? Fight me?" He reached for the ax, and she swung it at him. He jerked his hands back. "Oh, a feisty one." He grinned. "I like that."

Behind her, the form had finally pulled itself completely from the grave and was standing upright. It took a lumbering step toward them.

"That's right, girlie," Marko said. "Old Mr. Josh gonna make a quick meal out of your friends. He's hungry. And they got nowhere to run."

Sarah moved to shove Marko out of the way, but he grabbed hold of the ax handle. She held her grip, pulling it back with all her might. Marko was laughing. She could tell he wasn't using nearly all his strength to keep her at bay. He was toying with her. Her hands were slipping on the wet wood. She could feel the handle sliding in her grasp.

The Josh-thing was closer. Lightning flashed again and she could see the sinews holding its gray flash to the bones of its arms. It still wore the cargo shorts – now in tatters – that Sarah remembered from the photographs. It shuffled toward them, its unblinking eyes locked on them.

Screaming at the top of her lungs, Sarah coiled up and kicked between Marko's legs. She had no idea if her bare feet would be able to make an impact, but the man went down to his knees, groaning, his eyes clenched shut. Still he held onto the ax, his hands like a vice.

The Josh-thing was just feet away. She could smell it now – an odor like rotten leaves and singed hair. In a desperate move, she twisted to one side, and she and Marko fell to the soggy ground. She could not let go of that ax. If she did, she knew she would die.

Marko was struggling to sit up, but Sarah could tell the pain in his testicles had taken a lot of his strength. She crouched and rushed at him, rolling over him and landing on her back, her hands still tight around the ax handle. He was on his knees now. He pressed the handle against her throat. She couldn't breathe. She pushed back against him. White lights swirled through her vision.

Marko suddenly cried out, letting go of the ax and sitting upright.

Sarah scooted away from him, keeping her unbelieving gaze on the scene in front of her.

The Josh-thing had sunk its teeth deeply into Marko's shoulder. In the flashes of lightning, Sarah could

see blood flowing down the front of Marko's shirt. He
was screaming, hammering his fists at the thing's head.
The jaw and teeth began to work slowly and methodically, oblivious to the blows.

Still clutching the ax, Sarah got to her feet and ran
toward the cave.

14

Things had been quiet since Marko took Sarah.

David watched the shadows from the torch dance about the cave walls. He and Amy had discovered that by stretching toward each other as far as possible their hands could meet. They sat like that for some time with their fingers intertwined, listening to the roar of the storm outside.

He had given up trying to break out of the shackle around his ankle. The iron might have been old and rusty, but it was still strong enough that a man couldn't break it with his bare hands. He'd even tried pulling on the two bolts driven into the cave wall, and while one of them seemed a little loose, the other held tight.

They were going to die here. He knew it. It was so unfair. Just as he and Amy had found each other. Just as things had finally spun in the right direction for him and he was enjoying life. He was going to die like a gangland criminal. He wondered how they would do it.

Would they shoot them and dump their bodies at sea? Would they slit their throats? Or would they use them in one of their bizarre rituals somehow? He tried to ignore the hollow, sick feeling in his gut and think of some way he could bargain with them. What could he do, give them his boat? Promise to leave the island and never return or tell what they had seen?

Beside him, Amy sat still as a statue. She had stopped crying a little while ago. He could see her eyes in the firelight, though, still watery and glazed. He squeezed her hand and she gave him a weak smile. "If we get out of this, I'm never letting you out of my sight again," she said.

"It's a deal."

Fresh tears began to course down her cheeks. "All my life I've been searching for the right guy. Now that I've found you, it figures we'd be chained up in here like slabs of meat." She looked at him. "What do you think they've done with Sarah?"

"I don't know, babe."

"I'm really scared, David."

"I know, baby girl, I am, too."

Something moved at the entrance of the cave, and David felt his heart stop beating. And when the figure emerged into the light it took him a moment to realize the wet, scraggly, muddy thing in front of them was Sarah. She was holding an ax.

"Sarah!" Amy cried. "What happened to you?"

"We've got to get out of here," Sarah said. "They'll be coming any minute. And Josh and Emily are here."

Amy sat up. "They're here? Where are they? Are they okay?"

Sarah shook her head. "Oh, Amy, it's just so awful. There's no time to explain." She moved toward David, holding out the ax. "Can you use this to get yourself free?"

He took it from her and felt its heft. "Maybe."

He twisted and hoisted the ax above his head. The blade struck a glancing blow and bounced off the chain with a yellow spark. "Fuck!" This time he aimed for the bolt plate and the ax caught between the plate and the rock wall. He pried it toward him, and the loose bolt seemed to give a little.

"Keep trying!" Amy said.

He pulled harder, leveraging his feet against the rock. He could feel his muscles straining, could feel the ax handle starting to bend. The bolt slipped out with a puff of dust and fell to the cave floor.

"Now the other one!" Sarah cried.

David hefted the ax again and aimed for the spot between the bent plate and the rock. There was another spark as the blade hit the stubborn bolt. He pulled the ax loose and tried again. His chest and face were covered with sweat and his hands were slick and losing their grip. He swung again, and this time he felt the edge dig into the ancient metal. He took another swing and the blade bit deeper. "Almost got it!"

Suddenly, Amy screamed. David whirled around and tried to make himself believe what he saw.

It was a man, or what used to be a man, shuffling into the cave. The whitish skin, glistening from the rain in the torchlight, hung from its frame like tattered sails. Gray, sightless eyes sought them out and seemed to focus on Amy, who was closest. Its mouth and chin were covered in fresh gore that dripped onto its sunken chest. Worse, the yellow teeth worked up and down as if it still tasted whatever it had been gnawing on. Just like in the dream he'd had about Sarah at the top of La

Tour, the unseen thing chewing on her.

It lunged at Amy, and she screamed again. "David, do something!"

With one last desperate move, he brought the ax down on the bolt again. It cut deeper into the metal but the bolt still held fast. He lifted the ax up to Sarah. "Here!"

"What do you want me to do?" she cried, taking it from him.

"Swing at him. Try to hit him!"

Sarah took a step toward the walking corpse, the ax raised high. She swung the ax, screaming as she did so. The corpse lunged at her, snapping its jaws together.

David grabbed hold of the bolt plate, bending it up and back down. He could see the groove he'd made in the metal bolt expand and contract. If he could just work up enough fatigue in the metal to break it.

Behind him, Sarah took another step toward the thing coming at her. She swung the ax again, and it backed away, then rushed at her. "Josh!" Sarah said.

David turned and looked. Amy was looking, too. The thing stopped snarling and snapping and stood still, its white eyes aimed at Sarah. It tilted its head.

"Josh, I know what happened to you," Sarah said. "I know what they did to you. And Emily."

The thing became agitated. It swayed back and forth and held out its hands as if begging for answers.

David continued to work the cut bolt up and down. It was becoming easier now. Just a little bit more and he would have it.

"Emily's still here, Josh," Sarah said. "She's in the house. She's looking for you."

The corpse continued to sway. It snapped its teeth together and made a grunting sound.

In David's hands, the bolt broke in two and the chain clattered into the dust.

"Mama Alice is the one you want," Sarah was saying. "She's the one who did this to you. She has Emily."

The thing moved back and forth with uncertainty as if it was trying to decide what to do. It looked from Sarah to the mouth of the cave.

David leaped from the floor and pulled the ax from Sarah's hands, then drove it home into the corpse's skull. It fell without a sound. But as they watched, the fingers twitched, and the body sat up. Though the ax had crushed most of one side of its face, the shattered jaw continued to work. With a mixture of revulsion and curiosity, David could see the brain through a gaping hole in the thing's skull, shriveled and dusty as an old walnut.

"Hit it again!" Amy screamed.

David swung the ax a second time, striking the corpse in the neck. The head lolled to one side, held to the body only by a thin strip of dried flesh, the biting teeth clacking together relentlessly. The thing was getting to its feet. David swung again, aiming for the thigh. The ax struck home, and the body fell to the side, its femur now splintered. But still it was coming, struggling to stand. It didn't seem to understand that its legs could no longer support it. It reached out a hand, trying to pull itself forward through the dirt and sand on the cave floor. David hoisted the ax and brought it down on the corpse's wrist. The hand flew away and landed close to Amy's feet, where its fingers continued to writhe and claw at the air.

Sweat was pouring off David's body, and an ache gnawed in his shoulders. *Why wouldn't it die?*

Once more he brought the ax over his head and this time he aimed for the thing's emaciated back. The spine split in two with a sound that reminded him of slicing open watermelons back home in Indiana. The body fell to the cave floor, and the jaws snapped dangerously close to David's leg.

He aimed the ax for the head once more and knocked it loose from the body. He pounded the blade into the skull, smashing it beyond recognition. The jaw bone jerked once and was still. The legs and arms continued to move like a swimmer on dry land, but at least he had stopped those menacing teeth.

Amy stared at the thing writhing in front of her. "What. . . ?" she said. "What the fuck is *that*?"

Sarah stood with her hands over her mouth, watching the corpse. "It's Josh White. Or what's left of him."

Amy's mouth dropped open. "What happened to him?"

"I don't know," Sarah said. "They did something to him. Emily, too. Mama Alice has her in the house."

David pulled the ax from Josh's head and stepped toward Amy, his broken shackle trailing behind him. "Let's get you out of here."

Amy turned her head while David chipped away at the chain. Hers was coated in a thick layer of rust but was just as solid. This time, however, he was able to gather more leverage and the chain broke away after just a few hits.

He pulled her to her feet and she pressed her lips against his and pulled him so close he could barely breathe.

"Come on," Sarah said. "We don't have time for that." She led them out of the cave into the pouring rain.

"What do we do now?" Amy said.

"How far is it to the pavilion?" David asked.

Amy slung the wet hair from her eyes. "I don't know, not very far. But I have no idea which way we came. We'll never find it on our own in the dark."

He motioned toward the warm yellow lights of the house. "There."

"No!" Sarah cried. "We can't go in there."

"We can't stay out in this," David said. "She'll have flashlights. Tools to get these things off our legs."

"She'll kill us!" Sarah said. "You don't know what she's capable of."

David looked at her. "I've got an ax."

Light suddenly flashed into their eyes. "And I've got a gun," Mama Alice said.

David squinted into the brightness, shielding his face with his free hand. "Let us go," he said. "We're no threat to you."

"Oh, but you are," Mama Alice said. One hand held a flashlight and the other brandished an old pistol that looked like something from a pirate movie. There was no doubt in David's mind that the gun still worked. "Coming to my island, trying to make a fool of me, disrupting our sacred rituals."

"Marko raped Sarah!" Amy cried. "That's no fucking ritual! That's a goddamned crime!"

"Hush up!" Mama Alice told her. "What would you know about it? I know all about you, all the whoring around you do, all the men you been with. It's all the same to Bacalou. When his heir is born – "

"Shut up," David said with his jaw clenched. He wished he could see her clearly, see her eyes and which direction she was looking so he could make some kind of move. But all he could make out were the heavy raindrops coming down through the blinding beam of the flashlight. "We've all had it with your voodoo bullshit. Let Sarah and Amy go. I'll stay."

"No!" Amy said.

"That is ridiculous," Mama Alice said. "Sarah is the one we need. She is the chosen one. She will carry the seed of Bacalou."

"I'm not going to carry the seed of Bacalou," Sarah said evenly, stepping forward. "I'll see to that. I'll rot in hell first."

Mama Alice's voice was cold. "Should you destroy the seed of Bacalou, you'll *wish* you were in hell."

Sarah moved closer to Mama Alice. "Bring it, bitch."

The words were barely spoken before the flashlight flew from Mama Alice's hand and the beam caught the scurry of something leaping onto the old woman's back. Something that snarled and hissed and snapped.

David got just a glimpse of dead glistening eyes before the gun fired and his side exploded with pain.

15

At first, Amy was so startled by the figure leaping onto Mama Alice's back that she didn't notice the gun had fired. Only when she saw David slump to the ground and heard him cry out did she realize what had happened. She was by his side at once. "Oh, my God! David!"

He had balled up on the soggy ground, his hands clutching his side just under the ribcage. "I'm hit," he croaked. "Oh, God, it hurts."

She placed her hands on his and felt the hot trickle of blood through his fingers. "Oh, God!" She grabbed for the fallen flashlight. Sarah stood paralyzed, watching. Amy tugged on her hand. "Help me!"

Together they tugged David's shirt up and shined the light on the wound. The bullet had torn through the shirt and grazed the skin along his flank, leaving a swath of ripped flesh. It was bloody, but the wound didn't appear to be very deep. "We've got to stop the bleeding," Sarah said.

Amy handed the flashlight to Sarah and pressed her hands onto the gash. Blood continued to ooze between her fingers. David groaned. "Hang on, baby," she told him.

She could vaguely hear wet chewing above the sound of the rain. It was coming from just outside the periphery of the light. Sarah heard it, too. She aimed the beam of the flashlight toward the noise.

Mama Alice lay on her side, her eyes staring blankly up into the falling rain. The creature that had once been Emily White was crouched above her, gnawing on the woman's neck. A river of blood covered Mama Alice's throat and chest. Emily's white eyes glistened in the bright light. She hissed, and chunks of flesh fell from her teeth. After an eternity she lowered her head and tore into the bloody skin again with her mouth.

Sarah flopped onto the muddy ground beside Amy and leaned in close enough that Amy could feel her trembling. She knew Sarah's aversion to blood, and she wondered how she was managing to stay conscious. All Amy needed right now was a gunshot man and a passed-out friend to deal with.

"What's. . . what's going on?" David said, his voice thick.

"Nothing," Amy said, keeping her gaze on Emily. She was still feeding.

"Where's Mama Alice?"

"I don't think we have to worry about her anymore." She glanced down at him. His eyes were closed against the rain. "How you feel?"

"Shaky," he said through clenched teeth. "Still hurts."

"Sarah, the light," Amy said. Sarah shined the beam

down at David's side and Amy moved her hands. The blood was still flowing, but mixed with the rain she couldn't tell whether it was slowing down. "We've got to get him inside," she said. "Can you get up, David?"

"I don't know." He moved to sit up, then grimaced. "Oh, God, slower, *slower!*"

Sarah put a hand on her shoulder. "Wait."

Amy followed the beam of the flashlight. Emily was now standing over Mama Alice's body. Her wet hair and clothes hung limply against her gray skin. "What's she doing?" Amy whispered.

Sarah shook her head. "Where's the ax?"

"Here," David said, "beside me."

"Get it, Sarah," Amy said. "I'm not taking my hands off this wound."

Sarah slowly reached around Amy and pulled out the ax while keeping the light steady on Emily's blood-smeared face. Amy didn't shift her gaze from the thing's clouded eyes.

But Emily wasn't looking at them. She appeared to be looking *behind*, toward the sea in the blackness beyond. She stepped around the old woman's body and shuffled closer. Amy could sense Sarah lifting the ax to the ready.

Emily didn't acknowledge them. She stumbled past them and stopped when she reached another body further down. It was Marko. Part of his face appeared to be gone – chewed off. His dead eyes were still frozen with terror. Emily lumbered past him and stopped when she reached the disturbed grave. She reached a hand out toward it and made a sound like a muffled groan. A chill raced up Amy's spine. Emily lowered her arm and continued toward the sound of the crashing waves.

"What's she doing?" Amy said.

"She knows," Sarah said. "She knows what she is. Part of her is still in there."

Realization washed over Amy. "She's going to drown herself, isn't she?"

"She can't drown," Sarah said. "She can't die. Not until the flesh and bones are decayed and gone and the spirit leaves her."

Emily was far enough away now that the beam of the flashlight could only hint at what they were seeing. Emily strode into the water, struggling to keep her balance in the crashing surf. Amy and Sarah watched in silence as what was once Emily White moved farther and farther out, barely discernible in the weak light, until her head disappeared below the waves and they saw her no more.

Amy looked down at David. "Let's get him inside now."

☠☢☠

Inside Mama Alice's dusty, cluttered living room, Sarah and Amy cleared papers and books from an old natty sofa and laid David down. Now that they were out of the rain and had better light, Amy could see the bleeding had all but stopped. "How does it feel?"

"Stop asking me that," David said, his eyes closed. "It still hurts like fuck."

She knelt down and leaned into his face. "I think you're going to live."

He opened his eyes and looked at her. "You promise?" His eyes were so blue and intense, she wanted to lose herself in them and never be found.

"I promise," she said. She kissed him on the cheek. "Thanks for saving me back there."

He closed his eyes. "I think we're even now."

She looked back at the gash across his side. "I wish we could doctor this up some more, but I'm afraid to touch anything in this house."

"You might turn me into a frog."

"Or a rat."

Sarah sat down on the floor beside them. "So what do we do now?"

Amy shook her head. "Sit here and wait until morning, I suppose. Hope we can find our way to the path that takes us up to the pavilion." She looked at her. "Why don't you stretch out, try to get some rest. You've had a rough night."

Sarah touched her shoulder. "So have you."

Amy closed her eyes and leaned against the sofa and David's warmth. "I'll be all right." She reached out and took his hand. "I'll be fine."

☠🕷☠

By the time the sky turned a dusty pink, the rain had abated to a light drizzle and there had been no thunder and lightning for hours. The tide had deposited seaweed and driftwood on the rocky beach, but there was no sign of Emily's body. Amy remembered what Sarah had said last night, that she would go on until the flesh and bones rotted away, and she wondered if Emily would just keep walking through the sea until she was devoured by ocean life. It was a thought that made her blood turn to ice.

Sarah was curled up asleep on a rug in the middle of the floor. Amy found a dusty throw and tucked it around her. She had no idea how Sarah would be able to handle everything once this was over, and she cursed herself for fearing she would be Sarah's caretaker from this point forward. Going through the accident and losing Robert had been one thing. But this might be what finally pushed her over the edge.

David snored lightly on the sofa. She had checked his wound just as the sky began to lighten. It was crusted over with dried blood but didn't appear to be seeping. He was going to have a nasty scar. But it would be one they could tell their children about. She smiled and kissed his stubbled cheek. He mumbled something and began to snore again.

Out on the porch the air was heavy and wet and smelled of salt and fish. She sat on the edge of the porch and wondered what would be next. She had tried searching through the mess in Mama Alice's kitchen for a phone – either one of theirs or maybe Mama Alice's, but she found nothing. They were stranded. If they could get to the pavilion, maybe the hotel shuttle was still there and they could take it back to town. If not, one of them would have to take David's Honda to Ben Harbour and get the police. Provided they had sense enough to operate it. She hated to think of them trying to make the trek back to David's house on foot.

But surely someone would miss them. Someone would notice when David didn't show up to see about his boat. Someone would –

"Hallo?"

She sat up. That voice had come from the back of the house, toward the cave. "Hello?" she called.

She stepped off the porch into the wet yard and headed toward the sound. She saw the bodies splayed out beside the house and stopped. They looked worse in the light than they had during the night in the storm. A man in a red polo and khaki shorts was coming toward her, followed by several men in uniforms of navy pants and white shirts and caps. "Eric?"

"Amy? What has happened? Are you all right?

Where is Todger?"

"How did you find us?"

"David never came to inspect his boat this morning. I thought it was strange. I tried his cell but it kept going to voice mail. I called the inn and they told me you and Sarah checked out. I called the police then and we came looking for you at David's house. No one home but the cat, and I knew Todger wouldn't leave that cat in the house all day. I know then something is wrong. We got here and found his motorcycle parked up the hill at the temple."

Amy collapsed against him and felt the sobs coming long before they broke to the surface. Through gasps for breath she told him about their ordeal of finding Sarah at the ceremony, of being chained in the cave and attacked. "I'm sure it's still in there," she said. "It was moving when we left it."

Eric looked at the bodies of Marko and Mama Alice. "But. . ."

"Later," she said, leading to the front door. "Right now David needs help. Mama Alice shot him."

Eric followed her, a hand on her shoulder. "Everything gone be all right, girly-girl. Everything be all right now."

IV

EPILOGUE

It had been Amy who finally persuaded him to trim his schedule back to five days a week. At first it had been while he was recovering from the gunshot wound. Then after he healed he discovered he enjoyed spending two days with her each week, taking the ferry over to Nassau for the day or just relaxing at the house, and he had made a permanent change to his tour schedule. The loss of income was only negligible, and they got more time together. They were both happy, and that was all that mattered.

It had also been Amy who decided she was leaving the states and move in with him on St. Celine. "You need a woman to take care of you," she told him. They told themselves it was only for an extra two weeks while he recuperated, but before the time was up, she was already making permanent plans. The school on St. Celine needed a history teacher, and while Amy's background was in cultural anthropology and sociology, the school was desperate. The money was a pittance, but once Amy met the kids she was in love, and they with her. It was good for her, being with children, and it didn't take long before she was talking babies. David wasn't sure they were ready for that, but he hadn't completely dismissed the idea. They were still young, and there would be plenty of time to contemplate such things.

Today they had taken the catamaran out, just the two of them, and he had anchored just opposite where Mama Alice's house had stood. They sat in the captain's chairs, drinking beer and remembering that terrible night during the storm when they almost lost each other. The man who called himself "Marko" had turned out to be a Haitian voodoo priest named Jeane-Claude Brouard who was trying to infiltrate the voudon beliefs of St. Celine and other islands with his radical ideas of worshiping Bacalou, most of which involved ritualistic sex acts with female participants, willing or not. A manhunt had been going on for him throughout the Caribbean for years. How he had managed to get into Mama Alice's graces was a mystery, and now that she was gone, devoured by one of her own creations, it was destined to remain so. Three days after Eric and the police found the still animated remains of Josh White in the old cave, someone from Ben Harbour torched Mama Alice's house and property. No one tried to extinguish it, but many people from the town anchored in the bay to watch it burn.

David reached over and held Amy's hand. "You heard from Sarah lately?"

"Got an email yesterday. Fall semester's in full swing, she's staying busy. They got a replacement for me."

"Already?"

"Young guy, younger than Sarah, but she says he's interesting. And single."

"Look out."

"And she thinks she's probably sold her house. Gonna make a tidy profit on it, she says."

David sipped his beer. "Good for her."

"She wants to come visit in the spring."

"Bring it on."

They looked at each other and said "Bitch!" then broke down laughing.

"It'll be good to see her again," Amy said. "I was really worried about her going back, especially without me to look after her, but she's doing well." She looked at him. "She's *stronger*, you know what I mean?"

He nodded. He was stronger, too, as was his love for Amy. Some mornings he couldn't believe he was still waking up next to her, couldn't believe she'd taken on the role of manager for his tour business and first mate when the need arose. Couldn't believe how quickly she had adjusted to life on the island and the culture. Couldn't believe she had given up her career and everything she had back in Cedar Hill to be with *him*, a slightly pudgy Jimmy Buffett wannabe with a gunshot scar on his side and a cat who liked to drop dead lizards at the breakfast table.

Him, the luckiest man alive.

2

Hey Sarah!
So good to hear from you! Glad to know the college hasn't completely fallen to pieces without me. LOL. You tell that new cute little sociology instructor he'd better treat you right or he'll have to deal with me.

Talked it over with David and of course it would be OK for you to come visit over spring break. You're welcome to stay on our couch if you want, but something tells me you'll need a little more privacy. That's a whole six months away, though, so I'm sure you'll know something concrete before then.

Great news about your house! I know you were really bummed about that the last time we talked. You ever get your Skype working again by the way? I really miss our face-to-face chats. Remember that night we were drinking shots and trying to talk like pirates? LMAO. Anyway, your house. Where are you moving to? I know there are some really nice smaller houses on the other side of town from the school – retirement neighborhood mostly, but you'd probably fit right in. LOL.

Guess you probably heard the news that the Josh and Emily White case is officially closed now. DNA testing on the body in the cave proved it was Josh. Some divers found Emily's body just off the reef last week. ID'd her by her teeth. You know, sometimes it's like that whole thing was a dream. Did we really see what we thought we saw? Part of me wants to chalk it up to mass hysteria, but then the rest of me knows it was real. It was too horrible to be made-up.

GROSS!!! Seymour just brought in some kind of worm thing from outside. OMG, I've never seen anything like this before. I can't tell if it's a worm or some kind of baby snake. It's fat and red and it's making a noise almost like a kitten. God, that's the ugliest fucking thing I've ever seen! I'll take a picture of it for you with my phone and share the joy.

Write back when you get a chance, but I know you're busy. I can't wait to finalize plans for your visit. It will be so great to see you again!

Love,
A

Sarah closed out of her email and sat looking at the background on her laptop. It was the picture of Ben Harbour she'd snapped on the climb up to La Tour. She smiled. It would be great to be back on St. Celine, to see Amy and David again. She was glad they were happy and content. Things seemed to be going well for them.

She rolled the chair back from her desk and placed her hands on her rounded belly. Earlier today the baby was kicking, and she wondered if the two girls sitting on the front row during her lecture could see her stomach moving. She hoped so. She was proud to be carrying her child. Proud to be the chosen one. By April the baby would be old enough to travel, old enough to make the trip to St. Celine.

Sarah smiled. She couldn't wait to introduce him to the congregation.

ABOUT THE AUTHOR

Author and sometime banker **Will Overby** lives with his wife and a menagerie of cats and dogs in the rural lakes area of western Kentucky. Between dodging mergers and drafting policies he writes novels, including the crime thriller *The Killing Vision.* Connect with him on his website, www.willoverby.com, on Facebook, or follow him on Twitter (@Will_Overby).